# The Pixie Plot

# The Pixie Plot

Kate O'Brien

| Library of Congress Control Number: | | 2016915776 |
|---|---|---|
| ISBN: | Hardcover | 978-1-5245-9477-0 |
| | Softcover | 978-1-5245-9475-6 |
| | eBook | 978-1-5245-9476-3 |

**To order additional copies of this book, contact:**
Xlibris
800-056-3182
www.Xlibrispublishing.co.uk
Orders@Xlibrispublishing.co.uk
516754

# Contents

For Max and Harry

## PROLOGUE

# Cara

STEPPING UP WET wooden steps, Cara faltered. The sky was darkening already, casting the crumbling walls in deeper shadows. Water splashed onto her face and she realised her wool coat was soaked through. The rain was relentless, and her feet squelched in the mud as she strode up to the castle keep. The walls were taller and better preserved there, and so would shelter her from what was now an onslaught of rain and hail. She pulled up her hood, cocooning herself from the rain and stilled the storm inside her, breathing deeply and heavily. Her heart tightened with all the bitterness raging inside her. She was turning in to her grandmother, she realised, spitefully coveting what others had. 'Stop it, Cara. Pull yourself together!' She shouted into the rain and turned her face to the wet white stones.

Silver light cast down the grey slime of the old wet rock. It sparkled where the moonlight hit the quartz in the stone and dazzled Cara back in to the moment. How long had she been standing here?

Looking up through the funnels of raindrops, the moon blurred through her eyelashes and glowed milky and round against the night sky.

'Why can't I have a child? What did I ever do that was so wrong?' she sobbed, leaning heavily against the rock.

Sometimes, her thoughts would catch her out–so unlike her– lurking deep inside, waiting to leap up and out of her at a moment of weakness. She knew she would dote on a child-like Bette, she would spend every waking moment worrying, caring, loving, teaching, nurturing– all the things a good mother would do.

Sally was not a good mother. She was barely there for her daughter and it showed. The poor girl–staring out from her cot with dark, shadowy eyes–just begging for something to change. "You don't deserve her, Sally. If I had a daughter, I would love her too much and not too little.'

Speaking to oneself was a sure sign of madness, Cara was sure. Yet, it felt good shouting into the rain and Cara continued.

'Give me a child, Mr Moon!' she shouted, her hair thick with water and cold beyond comfort. Her body had started shivering, and her teeth had begun chattering, yet she no longer cared. Arms outstretched, the moonlight streaming through the rain now, and the wind whistling round the battlements, Cara shouted for one last time. 'Give me my child! You can have anything you like! Just give me a daughter to call my own!'

The air whistled round her ears, answering her call.

Sliding down the wall, her boots slipping in the mud, Cara found herself unceremoniously in a heap on the floor, her tights wet and muddy as the rain lessened and the wind stilled. Her little grey dress, proving little protection from this wild night, clung cold and wet.

'You silly thing,' she chastised, laughing to herself at the sheer stupidity of her actions–a single woman up here on her own, behaving like some mad, old witch. 'Get yourself home, Cara,' she groaned.

One day, she would have a child; of that she was sure. The child she often saw in her dreams–her long chestnut hair, and those wild green eyes–one way or another. Just not like this, wishing on a star in the pouring rain.

*Once upon a winter's night, under a low white moon, a young woman found a tiny baby hidden under a holly bush. The child was wrapped in nothing more than a sheet of silver muslin, and the woman took her in, blessed with this gift after not being able to have a child of her own for so long. The girl had been so tiny, so pale and waif-like, so otherworldly that the woman made it her life's work to keep her safe. At all costs.*

## CHAPTER I

# Holly

WRESTLING THE COVERS from her bed, she lay – eyes closed, her bare feet slipping in the oily mud of her dreams, her toes disappearing within a muddy whirlpool, sucking her down . . . down . . . Sticky all over, Holly's breath came ragged, her body hot. She saw her room was black around her and she reached hurriedly for the lamp on her bedside table–knocking her glass of water flying across the room in the process.

'No!' she gasped, as it clattered across the floor. Babies crying all around her as she came back in to the present, her mind spinning as she realised where she had been along. Pulling her blankets back over her skinny frame, she looked around rapidly, shaking the muddy whirlpool from her brain. She stopped. Had her mum or her brothers woken from their sleep? Could they hear the crying too?

Not a sound. Her warm breath unfurled into the icy air of the bedroom, and she pulled the covers protectively around herself. She had been having one of her dreams again: not the gentle, simple childhood dreams of long gone days, in which she could reflect on recent events, helping the brain sift the issues and dramas of the day. No. Holly's dreams were nothing like those dreams. She wished they were.

This was no good. Exams would be coming up soon. How little sleep could she exist on? She didn't need dark circles under her eyes for the 'beautiful people' at her school to comment on. Aside from their usual sneers towards the kids who hadn't quite made it into the popular circles that month, her appearance would, no doubt, give them cause for celebration.

'Oh Holly, have you seen a ghost? Your hair is quite standing up on end!'

'Holly, have you seen a ghost? Your skin is pale enough–you need some powder, my dear!'

'Oh Holly, have you seen a ghost? Your eyes are wide enough!'

Life at school was like living the story of Little Red Riding Hood, constantly running from the wolves. The usual uninspired comments from the rather uninspiring beautiful bullies came often. Holly could yawn them away on a good day; on a bad day, she planned colourful revenges which usually involved great cunning and death-defying stunts if she'd had the nerve or the power.

Quietly opening her bedside drawer, she removed the velvet notebook she kept there to record her dreams. Her best friend, Ethan, had suggested she write all these dreams down to see if there was any regular pattern, when she had confided in him a few months earlier.

Pages were covered in uneven rainbows of scribbles written on waking from night-time terrors. They described night after night of woods and whirlpools, starlight and full moons in short phrases, doodled drawings and random words as they came to her.

The wet mud, the midnight sky, and long tunnels which lay dusty ahead of her; the fear of losing her footing from the top of a high hill; sinking and swirling downwards; trapped in a tunnel's dead end once more and trying to scream while the dust caught in her throat. Every time in recent dreams she would then begin to fall until she would wake fighting her covers, wet and cold with fear and foreboding.

Flicking to the next blank page, she chewed her pencil. How did this dream begin? Let's go backwards, she decided. From waking up, let's step backwards through the dream as far back as I can.

*Right. Whirlpool, sucking me down to God only knows where. Like every dream I've had over the last few years. Losing my footing as the mound of earth turned down on itself, my feet scratched by roots as the earth falls away. The soil, the wet mud covering my legs up to my ankles before I fall and slide downwards, grabbing upwards at anything I can—roots, branches, plant vines . . .*

Her dreams were certainly starting to follow a pattern, she realised; and becoming more frequent.

This particular dream had followed a recurring theme, but different again—as they all were—if only very slightly. She poised her pen:

*I had been walking through woodland this time. Note that my feet are bare, as is usual in these dreams. There are trees all around me, autumn leaves of red, brown and butterscotch yellow. I am standing in what seems to be a clearing dotted with clumps of bluebells, white lily of the valley, and the odd red spotted toadstool peeping out from the leaf litter.*

*I am wearing a short woollen dress—charcoal grey with lace collar and cuffs, coarse against my skin.*

She flicked back a few pages to check.

Yes. Same dress, same bare feet, same landslide. Hair long, plaited.

Holly made a note. It was her but different—she looked different.

But how about before then? She had dreamed a walk through a woodland to a clearing.

*Where did I walk from? I was walking through the wood from somewhere. After nightfall, I walked through woodland I didn't know; I came upon this place quite accidentally. The trees were tall and thin but the wood was dense, and the leaves created a thin canopy layer through which I could barely see the moon. The moon. There was a full moon in the sky.*

*But how had I come to find the wood? Was it behind a wall? Or a hedge? Or a gate?*

No. Nothing else.

Holly stroked the burgundy velvet of its front cover before returning the book to its hiding place, after tying a black velvet ribbon around it with a bow. Not quite secure, but her little brothers would never dare undo it as they had not yet learned to tie their laces and so would not be able to cover their tracks.

The empty glass still lay on its side, its contents absorbed into the rug. She was relieved she had used a chunky tumbler—no tinkling sounds of broken glass to explain. Now, the incident would go by unnoticed. Wearily, she climbed back to bed and after turning off the light, closed her eyes. No more dreams now, she begged to herself or whoever might be out there to listen and take notice.

School tomorrow – a new term at her new school. It still felt like her new school even though she'd been there a year now. A full year since the big move, when everything had changed, and when these dreams had started. Just little ones at first, dreams of her walking around and around meeting people, or looking in mirrors—trivial stuff and nonsense—until these whirlpools had started three months ago.

As sleep crept over her once more, she drifted in to a deep dreamless state before her noisy brass alarm clock would wake her just a few hours later.

## CHAPTER 2

# Ethan

BEFORE HE KNEW it, Ethan was there again. A bus ride lost in an afternoon daydream was all it had taken. Away from home, his family, the noise of the school, and the drone of traffic all day long—all noise disappeared with every step as he ventured down the steep and dusty path: a yellowing trail down over a grassy bank, slipping on rough sandstone eroding beneath his feet. His boots left sandy imprints, more smudges than prints, as he struggled to keep the slow pace required to stay upright. A breeze flittering about his face, ruffling his chestnut layers, tickled his ears as it kept up this giddy game. The brightness of the day was fading now, his eyes growing accustomed to the grey around him. Beyond this place, a fiery sunset may well have marked the occasion more spectacularly, but here he was alone; in the dip of the valley no such luxuries were his.

Night-time would never be the greatest for Ethan, his eyes already straining to adjust to this half-light. A flap of wings above him—he jumped and slid the last few feet to the bottom of the countryside canyon. As his other senses started to compensate for his poor vision, the area came alive with sounds. Something scuttled by his arm and he pulled back cautiously—a grasshopper leapt suddenly out of the grasses. The jostling breeze had been left with the rest of the world as all seemed still from down in the canyon. The greying silhouettes of the trees seemed still from down here and Ethan marvelled at the journey he had made without much thought or planning. Daydreaming to the extreme, he smiled to himself. He lost hours at a time in this haze of a half-life.

Within a matter of days, the summer holidays would be over. School would resume its rigid timetable of lunchtimes and lesson times, break times and home times, a routine he secretly craved and escape from the chaos of home.

He knew that meant that he would be coming here after school at nights when Holly's mum hadn't invited him to theirs, and would bring snacks from the local shop, cooking anything he had afforded over an open camp fire, as he'd done so many times before.

Ethan collected dry sticks as he walked around the basin floor. The third cave he ran to held special importance to him and he dropped the sticks with a hollow clatter over the remains of grey ash from another fire days before. In the mouth of the cave, he sat and carefully stacked the twiggy branches, snapping protruding pieces and placing them within his pyramid structure. The rustling from his pocket revealed old newspaper which he stuffed into the centre of this structure and calmly rubbed dry sticks—bark on bark—until there's a spark, and then another, and the paper was lit.

Scraping the match along the sandpaper strip, a gentle whoosh gave a flame, his hand cupped around it protecting from the elements until it was safely pushed in to the newspaper base where the fire took hold and grew steadily. Ethan gently blew in to the flame until a gently licking fire warmed his hands and danced shadows across the cave walls.

His tea that evening had been two bread buns purchased on the way down here and a slice of ham the shopkeeper had slipped him as he often did these days. At one time, his pride refused such gestures, but his hungry belly no longer cared. His clothes hung from his shoulders, and his belt had now received yet another punctured buckle-hole. Cheekbones on adolescent males were neither cosseted nor admired, but any attention he received rarely extended to his looks. The kids at school were uninterested in this ghostly child unkempt hair dishevelled enough to pass for style, and dressed in black. He had always stayed comfortably outside the in-crowds and Holly was his constant.

Poking the fire, yellow flames licked up the dry twigs with an occasional crackle and Ethan rubbed his rough hands together over the top. Smiling, he remembered back to the first time he had come here, brought by his uncle, years before.

'Come on Ethan!' his uncle had called from inside the cave as Ethan warily stepped away from the safety of sunlight.

'Just a little farther, boy, you can do it!'

Ethan had breathed in deeply and ran, head down, determined to be wherever his uncle was. Visiting for occasional days peppered through his childhood, Ethan and his older sister would set out for adventures with their uncle and a short bus ride would deliver them, each time, to this spectacular series of caves set in this mixing bowl of sandstone, pushed down deep in to the ground, long forgotten.

'Me and your mum used to play here as kids,' he had once confided in Ethan, while the older sister kicked stones across the cave entrance. 'You coming, Bette?'

She had shaken the pale hair on her head from side to side, unspeaking as always, the scent of rose oil dabbed behind her ears the only real indication of her presence. Bette's fear of darkness and closed spaces would keep her at the cave entrance on watch under the white moon. A chance of fresh night air away from the angry jibes and dodged cuffs from their dad had brought her here. The stranger who stumbled home for supper each night before sleeping off a beery stupor in the armchair where he slumped, was no real match for this visit with her brother, yet being by these caves filled her with dread.

'Stay here then, my little moonbeam,' he had called. 'We'll not be long.'

In their own way, they were both glad to be with Uncle Harry. But the years of torment locked in the cellar under the stairs for petty misdemeanours had instilled in them a hatred of light-deprived, claustrophobic spaces, a punishment Bette and Ethan knew only too well.

Uncle Harry had taken Ethan's hand, that first time, and pulled him gently along the passage way as it narrowed and turned.

They had walked and walked; the tunnels twisting and turning this way and that, occasionally lowering and forcing them to stoop or crawl on hands and knees before opening up again into small chambers or junctions where left or right could mean reward or loss.

'At worst, we'll just arrive back where we started, Ethan,' coaxed Uncle Harry, sensing Ethan's bravery deserting him for a moment. 'But in a moment, I will take you to a place previously visited by one person, and one person alone.'

His eyes had sparkled, full of secrets and wonder; Ethan's stomach had tightened in excitement. Being here, like this, had been the most daring and memorable time in his short life so far and each time he remembered, he lived every heart-stopping moment. The tunnel had reduced; forcing them on hands and knees, then above them appeared a hole which Ethan stretched up to.

'Reach up and pull yourself up onto the shelf. You'll see it, son, be strong now.'

Standing, Ethan realised that the cave they had stepped into was no wider than the bedroom he shared with his sister, yet its ceiling stretched up and away in to the sky above. He pulled himself up onto a ledge and gasped. Blue and purple glints twinkled all around, and from the ceiling, stone icicles hung majestically at intervals while a gentle silver ebbed from the walls allowing them to see every inch of his uncle's secret space. Swinging his legs up, he stood in this space holding his arms tightly around him. He could barely breathe. His stomach hard and his breath tight in his throat, he realised that he had never before seen anything like this, not even in the few storybooks he treasured.

'Here we are in the centre of our universe,' Uncle Harry had announced as he scrambled up to join him; his voice echoing around and around the natural cathedral of rock, its ceilings and floor studded with fine stalactites and stalagmites.

Climbing out in to the moonlit night, they had found Bette curled up sleeping, where they had left her.

'Wake up, Bette', Ethan had whispered shaking the skinny frame of his sister. 'Wake up, Bette!'

Unable to wake her, Uncle Harry had carried her away from the caves and she, in time, had stirred.

'Hello, sleepy—you were fast on,' their uncle laughed as he put her down.

'You were such a long time—I was afraid', she sobbed, 'and I thought you'd left me there.'

'We were no time at all, little Bette. Dry your eyes now, there's a good girl.'

Ethan hugged his big sister, the scent of roses filling his nostrils and wiped the streaky tears from her cheeks. 'It was beautiful in there, Bette. You'd have loved it. We'll have to go back.'

'Not without me you won't,' said Uncle Harry said. 'No place for kids on their own—you'd never find your way out. But I will bring you again, mark my words. I need to be seeing my favourite niece and nephew more regularly. We'll come next time I'm up and then we'll take you too, Bette. Okay?'

Bette had nodded, her dirty pale face solemn and sad.

And ever since he was old enough to come alone, since Uncle Harry gave up them, Ethan came here to find peace and tranquillity, calm and safety—away from the brawling fists of the man his mother had married, away from the mum who gazed with hazy love out at him when he kissed her goodbye, and release from the memories of the precious sister he lost soon after.

## CHAPTER 3

# Cara

SALLY HADN'T ALWAYS been this way. Cara Adams remembered a time when Sally was the one she ran to at any time of trouble. Their teenage years had been a hysterical rollercoaster throughout, their friendship solid and sacred. Their friendship had survived their attending of different colleges – Sally in York and Cara in Scarborough – both teacher training and growing up, ready for adult life.

Cara had watched her friend as their lives took such similar paths for a while, each teaching at local schools: Cara at the school her children all attended, while Sally taught Science at the secondary school up the road.

When Sally left work to have a child after one year of teaching, the dreams of a teaching career went on hold. Little Elizabeth was beautiful and now Sally was a mother, her life took a different path to Cara's. They grew apart in some ways but Sally would visit Baby

Bette and compare stories. Cara had prayed and wished for a child of her own, yet none came.

Sally rarely left the house, much to Cara's dismay, yet Sally didn't seem to mind any more. She seemed resolved to do as her husband bid, and be the best she could at being a wife and mother. Her husband Daniel was a strange one though. A tiny blonde-haired man whose nervous eyes darted out at Sally from behind rectangular glasses, whispering instructions to keep Sally by his side.

'Really don't think you need to go out today–the house needs cleaning.'

'If you've got spare money to have coffee with Cara, you can give it to me to get petrol for the car.'

'If you have a spare hour, I've got paperwork that needs sorting–Cara can see you another day.'

Slowly and surely, Cara and Sally saw less of each other as Sally became a reluctant housewife and mother to this small child. Sally would help when she could, but worried about the dirty house and the dirty cot, the child left alone in a wet nappy all day, and Cara could see her friend wasn't coping.

Sally even called on the community nurse to help and eventually one came and sniffed about the place. On one particular visit after the stern community nurse had come to check on the infant, she had taken Cara aside and spoken of Sally's neglect of her daughter.

'The room is airless and damp,' she had sniffed, inspecting the dusty bed sheets in the cot.

Hurriedly pushing the small top window open, Cara had smiled and tried to put it down to forgetfulness.

'It isn't your job to do a mother's job for her. The child is neglected. I can feel her sadness.'

'I called you to help her. I just help when I can–Sally is doing her best. Just see if there's anything the child needs and maybe check in on Sally too.'

'Well, you say that, my dear, but I'm sure all your friend really needs is to wind the clock back and be childless–not listening to a screaming baby all day long.'

'She tries to be a good mum,' Cara had said unsteadily, not sure if she truly believed this herself. Not all women made good mothers after all.

'But, she's not, you say?' the nurse had noted, scribbling furiously in a little spiral bound book.

'I never said that,' Cara had frowned.

'But such a shame you are without your own little Bette,' the nurse had cooed.

'My time will come, I'm sure.'

'All you need to do is wish hard enough, my dear. Close your eyes and make that wish. Maybe both yours and Sally's dreams will come true.'

The woman was clearly potty and Cara had shaken her head and walked downstairs to check on Sally, whose hands were soapy in a sink of hot water as she tried to clear away the mess of a week's washing up and baby bottles.

'She's a strange one, the nurse,' Sally had whispered. 'Have you seen her before?'

'No, she said she's new–the last one wasn't quite as snooty.'

'She's looking at Bette now. Why don't you go up and talk to her? You need to find out why she's crying.'

'You're right,' Sally nodded. 'She just scares me. Makes me feel like I'm a rubbish mum. I am trying, Cara. It's just so hard.'

'I know,' Cara had smiled. 'But you're in charge of that little life upstairs and you need to do everything you can to keep her safe and happy. I'll help you but you've got to try and get on top of things a bit too.'

Putting on a pair of white leather gloves, the nurse appeared in the doorway. 'All done and dusted, Sally. Cara? I'll take my leave.'

Cara had nudged her friend, gently. 'Do you want to ask anything, Sally?'

'Is she okay?'

'The baby is upstairs. She's calm and quiet. Go and check on her when you're ready.'

And Sally remembered that day, how the child almost at once had stopped screaming out for her mother.

'Well whatever you've done, it seems to have done the trick.'

'Don't thank me, Sally. Thank Cara.'

Cara had frowned at the nurse–she remembered that now–as the unsmiling woman had winked back in response.

Later that week, Sally had turned up to look after the child, as she did most evenings, to a quiet house and a calm Cara.

'Is Bette okay?' she had asked, following her friend to the drinks cabinet.

'Sleeping, I think,' Sally smiled. 'I've just been up to her–she seems much calmer today.' The clink of ice in her glass as she poured tonic in to the gin was the only sound in the house.

'Can I pop up and see her?'

'Be quiet, Cara—she's sleeping.'

As Cara and Sally tiptoed in to the room, the child's deep brown eyes stared out from between the bars.

'Hello Bette, my little darling,' Cara had whispered. 'How's my favourite little girl?'

But the child barely looked up. She didn't seem to recognise her.

'Do you think she's okay, Sally? She's really quiet.'

'She's fine, Cara. She stopped crying and that's the main thing. I wonder if she's been a bit off it you know, she seems fine now.'

Cara had felt the baby was far from fine. Her colour was more clay than flesh and she was clammy to the touch. To make sure, Cara had called the health visitor back the following day.

On her return, the nurse said there was nothing to worry about, that maybe the child had had a bout of colic and Sally should try and get some rest. Cara felt concerned but continued her visits every few days.

'I suggest you keep your opinions to yourself,' the health visitor whispered. 'You don't want to fuss over nothing and upset the apple cart now, do you?'

'Which apple cart would that be?' asked Cara, never a big fan of metaphors. The tiny wiry woman had pursed that tight mouth of hers and shaken her head.

'Isn't it about time you were getting a child of your own?' she purred, placing her notes carefully back in her brown Gladstone bag.

'I've – I've not been lucky enough, that's all. I hope one day . . .'

At this, the nurse's piercing blue eyes settled firmly on Cara. 'My dear, our children come to us when they're good and ready. You just wait and see. You will soon be granted your child after helping your friend in this way. I am sure of it.'

'Such a relief about little Bette. Thank you for your help.'

The nurse had smiled, yet her eyes had remained harsh with the beady look of a hawk.

'My duty and my pleasure. Her mother has more uninterrupted drinking time ahead of her now that she has a quiet child.'

'Sally loves Bette—she does her best.'

'Indeed.'

And with that, the nurse had gone, the front door clicking shut behind her, leaving Cara open-mouthed and alone.

## CHAPTER 4

# Holly

MORNING CAME ALL too soon for Holly. She rubbed her eyes and made her way out onto the landing, pulling her thin robe around her. Stepping into the next room, twin beds full of crumpled bedding, Holly made her morning announcement.

'Boys! Good morning, guys! Rise and shine!' She heard little groans seep from the woollen blankets and took that as proof that her task was accomplished.

'Breakfast for anyone dressed for school in ten minutes!' she called, before shutting herself back in her room and pulling on the grey uniform laid out on the chair by her dressing table.

She heard the boys jumping around next door, thudding as they jumped from bed to bed, and squealing as they chased each other around.

'Good morning, Mum,' Holly smiled, pushing the door ajar. She lay asleep, tiny in the big double bed she had shared with her dad until everything had changed and they'd found a new way of life. 'Good morning, Mum,' she repeated. 'I'll bring you your cup of tea.'

Downstairs, the old wooden table lay set for breakfast. Holly poured porridge oats into the pan waiting on the stove, and then carefully poured out three cups of milk before stirring them into the mixture. The stove lit, she stirred the liquid gently in a clockwise direction until the spoon slowed down and the thick silky mixture steamed hot from the pan. Cups of tea and bowls of hot porridge sent smoky spirals skyward as the clatter of shoes on wooden stairs indicated the boys' arrival. After cutting a couple of apples into shiny green and cream segments for the centre of the table, Holly joined them.

'Where's the syrup, Hol?'

'Where's the sugar? Can I have some cold milk, Holly?'

As Holly moved the requested items to her brothers' reach, she mouthed 'pleeeeaaase!' as a gentle reminder, only releasing the prizes when they spoke the magic word.

The twins ate quickly, their eyes never leaving the bowl until each was bare and as clean as they had been not seven minutes earlier.

Dressed with collars in and out, trousers back to front and socks on in varying degrees, Holly talked the boys through a redressing before they were permitted to take out their shoes ready for polishing.

Tom and Jack had learned their task and Holly felt able to let them clean their own shoes. As she heard the *shush, shush, shush* of the brushes polishing up the black cream in fast rhythmic sweeps, she smiled and returned to her brothers.

'Not bad at all, Jacob. Not bad at all.'

Jake's milky grin said it all. His knuckles were black with boot polish and the newspaper laid out to protect the kitchen floor was covered in irregular shiny black shapes, but he had polished his own boots which meant he had helped Holly by doing his job well.

'What about mine, Holly? Will they do?'

'Oh, yes, Tom, I would think so. But how you got polish across your forehead is beyond me!'

Wiping a cold wet dishcloth across his brow brought about frozen shrieks.

'Hold still, Thomas, hold still!'

'Holly, no! It's perishing cold, stop now! Holly, stop!'

'Are you excited to be back at school, Jake?' Holly laughed. These boys got dafter; every day they grew larger and she loved them for it.

'Yeah, Holly–but I hope we don't get nits again!'

'Eurgh!' squealed Tom, bashing his shoe noisily on the floor. 'Not again. I don't want any more pets!'

'I'm sure you'll be fine, and remember what Mum said, head lice only like clean hair; so you must have been a very clean class last year.'

Shaking their heads, the boys scratched before throwing their bowls and spoons in the sink.

'Careful, boys–please place your dishes *carefully*!' Holly snapped. Chaos. Absolute chaos. She breathed deeply and wiped the table of cereal debris and milky splodges before following the boys back upstairs.

'Teeth!' she yelled as a mock order. She heard the boys clamber noisily into the bathroom where toothpaste sat squeezed on brushes, left by their mum the night before.

As Holly entered the tiny space, she found the boys sword-fighting with loaded toothbrushes.

'No!' she yelled, grabbing hopelessly the flailing arms and white gunky splashes.

The boys stopped in their tracks as Holly shouted again.

'NOOOOO!' Holly's white school shirtsleeve was now striped with sticky pink toothpaste, matching the sticky stripe in Jake's hair.

Damp flannel in hand, Holly rubbed and rubbed the hair as best she could, combing out the residue, ignoring his screams.

Her shirt fared less well and although rubbed frantically, the sticky mark just grew less sticky yet larger and greyer than ever.

Counting very slowly to ten, Holly went to her room and dug out a grey wool jumper, misshapen yet far better to wear than brave school with a marked shirt. It would surely be a fate worse than death.

As Mum came out on to the landing, the three children looked quite orderly and ready for school.

'What happened to your shirt?' Mum asked, rubbing Holly's arm affectionately.

'Jake happened. That's what,' she growled, pulling on the grey sweater, more annoyed at her own mood now than the grey minty mark on her hidden sleeve.

'Thank you, Holly,' Mum smiled.

The twins threw their arms around Mum and shouted their morning greetings.

'Come on guys, time to go!' Holly said brightly, carefully concealing any hint of a mood. 'Bye Mum, love you!'

## CHAPTER 5

# Bette

**B**ETTE WAS A quiet, pensive child. She would speak only when spoken to, and she worried the teachers at school with her tired, worried face. Life at home was all she knew, but she wished her Dad would shout less and her Mum would smile more. Maybe the new baby would help make things better, although Bette knew her Dad was not keen on this new addition to the house. Dad didn't like noise. Or mess. And the new baby had brought both.

Bette escaped to school every day and loved the calm and quiet classrooms, the smiley teachers and the distraction of writing, reading and arithmetic, even though she found all three difficult. She wished Mum would read with her more and help her with her homework, but had stopped asking.

Wednesday was her favourite day of the week as she stayed behind for Green Wellies Brigade, a long-standing tradition at her school. Tonight, she had been given the task of weeding the bottom area of the Healing Garden, further on from their usual patches of herbs and flowers. The children stood in defeated huddles, their shoulders down as they realised their evening task.

'We're not allowed down there, Miss,' one child had ventured before being told it was her place to listen and do as she was told.

Mr Bartholomew had enlisted the help of another teacher, Miss Trench, to cover Miss Larch's class that day. An older member of staff who the children had had very few dealings with, Miss Trench was a nosy, strange little woman who the children stayed well clear of. She eyed the children with a hawk-like curiosity and her chin pointed accusingly at anyone who dared to raise their hand. She had been given the job to lead the group that evening and had announced that they should clear the weeds and wild flowers at the bottom of the garden.

'We don't normally work down here, Miss Trench,' the group had moaned, keen to continue with the planting and tidying of the lovely gardens they were used to.

'Nonsense,' Miss Trench had sharply replied, snipping at the unruly children the way she hoped to be snipping at the unruly weeds in a few minutes' time. 'This will be quite the surprise for Mr Bartholomew when he returns from his meeting.'

'But he says we're not allowed,' Bette had whispered, her hand jabbing up and down nervously. 'He said children mustn't come down here, Miss Trench.'

'Children, Bette, are to do as they are bid. And I bid you to work in the gardens today. What is special about today, Bette?'

'Nothing, Miss Trench.'

'Today, you are no longer a little child. Today is your birthday, is it not? I've been looking at your records.'

'Yes, Miss Trench.' The old lady had closed in on Bette and circled her for a moment. 'So you, my dear, are no longer a child. You will work at the gates, my dear. Children cannot work down there, but you are not a child anymore.'

'Mr Bartholomew told me never to stray past the garden. You just don't know. Shall I go and get one of the other teachers? They'll explain.'

'Obstinate too? Obviously getting ahead of yourself, in this twilight hour between child and . . . other. And is that . . .' Miss

Trench sniffed, her mouth curved down in a sneer, '... perfume you're wearing? Getting ideas above your station, young lady?'

'My mother's. I wear it on special days.'

'Well you'll do well to remember your place. You will do as you are bid. Are you afraid? Are you still a child after all?'

Bette looked back to her classmates, a few of whom were anxiously glancing in her direction before getting on as they had been ordered to. The children had quickly taken their places, with no discussion and certainly no arguments. This strange teacher, drafted in to cover the lovely Miss Larch, was a far cry away from the usual teachers at this school and they knew better than to question her. Bette walked alone to the gates. Digging at the bluebells and forget-me-nots under that wrought iron gate, she sobbed quietly, knowing no one would hear her as Miss Trench in her wisdom had placed the girl as close to the woodlands edge as was possible and had left her alone. Bette knew she was being punished and diligently went about clearing the weeds, hopeful of Miss Trench's praise at the end of the session. Her birthday had been forgotten by her mother and now sneered at by this mean teacher. Bette felt lost and alone. The strong smell of the yellow weeds tickled her nose, her sad coughing the only sound she made. Drowsy and forgotten, Bette worked until her fingers bled and her head ached.

## CHAPTER 6
# Sally and Cara

W HEN HER DAUGHTER, Bette, was late, Sally had assumed the club had continued a little later than usual. The girl often walked home alone these days to a cold house and a mother asleep on the bed upstairs. She seemed unworried when Cara popped by to check on Ethan after school–a routine Cara had insisted on since the baby was born. Cara liked to check in on her friend and make sure Bette had got home safely. Her little Holly came everywhere with her now and today was no exception.

'It's just me–Bette? Sally?'

The door slammed behind her and she peeped in to the kitchen. Cereal boxes and a milk carton sat out on the table along with remnants of the morning breakfast. A black and white cat jumped down and wound herself around Cara's ankles.

Cara sighed and smiled sadly. She stroked Holly's hair and hugged her tightly. 'Let's get this place tidied up shall we?'

'Sorry, Cara, I must have nodded off.' Sally staggered downstairs, fully dressed yet sporting bed hair and smudged mascara.

'Where's Bette, Sally? Is she not home yet?'

Sally walked past them, scratching her head. 'She has a club so she'll be home at 4 pm Do you want a cuppa?'

'It's after five, Sally.'

Sally pressed the switch on her kettle. 'Right. I'll kill her when I see her. What's she playing at?'

Cara half-walked, half ran to the school, her heart pounding in her chest, her fingers gripping the pram handles tightly. Holly lay silently in the pram as they hurried together. Sally followed closely behind, her pram rattling noisily across the paving stones, Ethan quietly protesting. As they ran through reception, Cara forced herself to breathe calmly and put on as best a front as she was able. She could be wrong about Bette. She hoped she was. 'Hello Mr B. I'm here to collect Bette. She normally walks home, but she's not turned up.'

He frowned and adjusted his collar, straightening to meet her gaze. 'Bette? Miss Larch was not in today–a family illness, I believe. Green Wellies Brigade was cancelled. Miss Trench took the class and I'm sure it finished at the usual time.' He motioned down the corridor. 'Shall we?'

Miss Sharp was summoned.

'Can you mind these two while we attend to something, please Miss Sharp?'

'It will be my pleasure, Mr Bartholemew. They're safe with me.'

Cara glanced anxiously at Holly sleeping in her pram before being hurried out of school down to the Healing Garden, where they found Miss Trench pushing handfuls of garden rubbish steadily in to a large silver bin.

'Miss Trench . . .'

As he spoke, his eyes had scanned the area at the bottom of the garden and this time said her name somewhat louder. 'Miss Trench! What have you been doing?'

'Haven't they done a lovely job, Mr Bartholomew? They have cleared the whole area in the hour we put aside for the job. Such hard workers, Mr Bartholomew. You have trained them well.'

Sally gasped as she saw this woman in front of her. Older, but unmistakeable.

'We will talk later about this, Miss Trench. Bette does not appear to have arrived home so this is of the utmost importance. Did Bette leave with the other children?'

Miss Trench pinked and slowly peeled off her gardening gloves, deliberately averting her eyes from the anxious stare of Cara and Sally. 'I – I sent them home. I stayed here and they all went together.'

'And Bette?'

Her glance at the bottom gate betrayed her and she felt Mr Bartholomew tense.

'As I've already told you, the children went home. Over an hour ago.'

'Do I know you?' Sally whispered, stepping tentatively towards Miss Trench.

'We need to inform the appropriate channels, Miss Trench. I suggest you make the necessary calls.'

'What have you done?' Cara's voice quivered as she stepped towards Miss Trench. Miss Trench took a step back and steadied herself on the bins.

Miss Trench shook her head at Cara; her lips pursed tightly before turning quickly on Sally and pointing her finger accusingly. 'And what time did you realise Bette was gone?' she asked, her voice steady and cruel. 'I released the children at four o'clock. So where were you? That is more likely the question the police will be asking!'

'Highly inappropriate, Miss Trench,' the head teacher gently muttered. 'Please wait for me in my office.'

Sally had not taken her eyes off this woman since they had arrived at the Healing Garden. Her hands now red from the repeated wringing, her voice shaking as she gasped. 'I know you from somewhere. We've met before.'

'Not the time, Sally. Come on let's go up to school.'

Cara had placed her; she recognised that look and that manner from a decade before.

'Has been missing for well over an hour, my dear. Not quite mother of the year now, are we?'

Sally shook her head. 'We need to find Bette. This is terrible.'

Miss Trench rose a little too quickly and walked towards the school building. Cara ran after her.

'Where is Bette? What has happened? Please don't go—we need to find her.'

'Don't spoil things for yourself, Cara. It has all worked out as we planned.'

'I don't know what you're talking about–.where is she?'

'Back from whence she came. All wishes have a price, my dear.'

Sally ran to the gates of the woods, its elm trees lined beyond it in the twilight. 'Do you think she went in there, Mr B? Why would she go there after everything you said?'

'Children know not to go out of the school grounds, Sally. Bette is a sensible young lady. Let's go up to school and see what we can sort out. Try not to worry.'

Ashen faced, Cara had half-walked, half-ran to the school office where calls were being made, pulling the dazed Sally along with her.

Cara and Miss Trench followed behind. 'I don't know what you're saying, Miss Trench. This is no time for games.'

'Oh, this is no game, Cara. Nothing but an end to a chapter. You made a wish. The wish was granted and payment is made.'

'What payment? Oh my god, Miss Trench–what have you done to Bette?'

'I will come to see you tonight at the house. But I suggest you remember your sweet little Holly and how she was your sweetest wish. Every wish has a price.'

'Oh my god–I know who you are. You were Bette's nurse when she was a baby.'

'Payment was partly made a decade gone. This is merely the end of things. Just remember that. Bette is merely returning from whence she came. Try not to worry, my dear. All is well and Holly remains with us.'

'What is this?' Cara gasped through her fingers, tightly pushed over her own mouth, not daring to join up the dots. 'What do you know of Holly?'

'That poor child, Cara, do you remember? How neglected she was? Sally was not fit to be a mother. But you were. You were desperate for a child of your own. Such a sad, childless woman.'

'I don't know what you are implying, Miss Trench.'

They walked in silence up to school. Sally and Mr Bartholomew had long gone inside.

'Where do you think Holly came from, Cara? You never handed her in to the local children's home, did you?'

'No, because she was mine. I knew she was mine.'

26

'Precisely. And why was she yours, my dear?'

Cara stumbled and steadied herself on the wall of the school. They both leaned against it and looked back down towards the gardens from where they had come.

'Because I wished for her. She was mine because I wished for her.'

'All magic has its price, my dear. You merely helped Holly come to you. Your payment is not yet made in full, Cara, my dear. Do not lose sight of your prize now, Cara. The worst is behind you.'

'Where is Bette, Miss Trench?'

'Where she's been all this time, Cara. Remember this:

*'These changelings live a whispered life*
*Once human babes are gone*
*Two lives we take, your freedom make*
*The moon child will live on.'*

Sally burst out of the school. 'Cara – we've got to go. I need to be back before Dave gets home. He's going to kill me.'

'What did the police say?'

'They're on their way to the house. I can't believe this, Sally. I need a drink. Will you come back with me?'

Sally looked to Miss Trench who nodded, formally. 'You go with her. She needs you. We will talk again.'

Sally's head played over and over the conversation she'd had with Miss Trench all those years ago. How could she possibly have anything to do with Bette's disappearance?

'Come on Cara. Hurry!'

The two ran home to find the police car parked outside the rundown fencing and the overgrown weeds that framed the front of Cara's house.

'Did you recognise her?'

'Who?'

'That Miss Trench—she was your nurse when you had the kids, both times.'

'Don't remember, Cara. But she's a teacher—you must be mistaken.'

'Miss Trench . . . I'm sure of it. She'd have been ten years younger, though, as we all were. Perhaps I am wrong.'

'Can we just focus, Cara?' Sally sobbed, her shaking hands pulling her thin coat around her slight frame. 'We need to find Bette. I don't give a damn who that woman is. I just need to find my daughter.'

Within the week, blue bells and forget-me-nots had been reinstated in the borders surrounding the bottom wall and gate, and Miss Trench left the school. A search of the area was made but Bette was never found.

## CHAPTER 7

# Holly and Ethan

I T WAS A short walk to the school gates from home and the boys raced to the green railings, both grabbing the iron railings in unison.

'Have you got your dinner money, boys? The envelopes are in your book bags, remember?'

The boys ran back to Holly who did a quick infantry of their necessary equipment, first day back.

'Dinner money?'

'Check.'

Tom began laughing as Jake took them through the infantry. 'Underpants, check. Uniform, check. Book bag, check. Dinner money, check.'

'Kisses?'

'Check!' they shouted as they each kissed Holly's cheek before screaming and running off towards the school building.

'You're both crackers!'

She followed them in to school for the first day at the junior school, as she had no idea how they'd ever get to the right classroom without her. They were an insane double act, as hilarious as they were annoying, yet their awareness of the outside world often took second place to their inadvertent comedy routines.

Holly looked around this tiny school, once a labyrinth of a place that her five year old self got lost in, its white corridors and wooden cloakrooms the same at every turn. She had loved that school, with its warm waxy polish smell and crackling white-hot radiators where the frozen milk stood in little rows as the ice thawed away.

'Boys, come on, coats on here,' she called, pulling them gently towards the cloakroom to find their names on the pegs.

'We're here, Tom. Look!'

'I'm next to you–how perfect is that? T-O-M. They're capitals, Holly, that's because we're a whole year older!'

'J-A-C-O-B. Can you read mine, Tom?'

As they practised their letters, Holly peeled off coats and gloves, carefully pushing gloves in to pockets in the vain hope they may manage not to lose them on the first day back.

In the new classroom, blue display boards covered with Roman soldiers on one side and parts of a flowering plant–a colourful cross section with simple labels–on the other. The sets of milk cartons wrapped in plastic didn't look quite as inviting as those cold little bottles of milk she remembered as they sat in a basket by the door.

'Good morning, boys,' the teacher smiled as Holly shepherded her brothers closer.

'This is Tom, and this is Jacob,' she started.

'Jake,' Jake reminded her with a sharp poke on the bottom for effect.

'Sorry, Jake. This is Jake–where do you want them?'

The teacher looked young and a little nervous, but smiled brightly; her blonde bob bobbing as she spoke. 'Hello, Jake. Hello Tom. My name is Miss Larch,' she grinned. 'You just choose a reading book from the library shelf there and sit at a table of your choice.'

'Really, Miss?' Tom asked, '– any table?'

'Any table, but chatterboxes may have to be moved to a table of my choice. I'm just warning you!'

The boys smiled at each other and hugged Holly round the legs. 'Bye Holly. See you after school.'

'Okay, boys, love you, see you later. It'll be me or Mum picking you up, okay?'

'Okay, Holly . . .' and they were gone, into the wriggling mass of knee-high people choosing their books in the library corner.

Holly had loved her time at that school, when learning was sprung upon you through playing and doing, and making and choosing. A photo looked down at her from a nearby cabinet and she stopped. His twinkling green eyes smiled down at her from ten years ago–Mr Bartholomew, her favourite teacher, and now the head teacher of the school. A giant of a man with floppy silver hair and bushy eyebrows to match, he looked after the conservation area at the school and ran The Green Wellies Brigade of which she played a part. Every week, two or three lunchtimes were spent digging and sowing, weeding and pruning the gardens beyond the school grounds. There grew vegetables all year round, as he knew just which to plant in harmony with the seasons; while Holly's favourite garden was the Healing Garden, as it was called. She enjoyed weeding and caring for all the plants there. She could almost smell the lavender and rosemary again as she remembered tending each row in that secluded little spot behind the school.

Over the years, as he could no longer manage the physical work of the garden, he had ensured that the Healing Garden would remain there and would be tended by future teachers at the school, a job which had been continued over the years. She would have to ask the boys to take her down there and show them what she had done there all those years ago.

Time was getting on. Holly would have to race now if she was going to make it before registration. She may have to speed things up a bit to make it without rushing. How she wished she'd worn a warmer coat. The summer seemed to have evaporated overnight, leaving a damp, cool, mist all around. Miserable grey weather. That time, before Autumn really kicks in with its crisp coldness all around and crunchy dry leaves carpeting the pavements and brightening the trees with their red and gold transformations. Holly's favourite time of year, by far, was Autumn.

She wondered what this term would bring. How was it that each year, school felt so new and nerve-wracking even though she'd been going since she was five years old? Holly prepared herself to move in to swift mode. Ready –

'Hey, Holly!'

'Oh, hello Ethan.'

'You all set?'

'As I'll ever be. What about you?'

'Nothing to worry about, sunshine. I'll smash it.'

"Course you will, Ethan. There's Drama Club, remember? You'll audition for the winter production, won't you?'

'Not sure, Holly, my love,' he laughed. 'I take it you've not heard then?'

Holly stopped. 'Heard what?'

'The Pageant are taking over. They've decided it's now cool to be actors and they're going to hijack the auditions. Don't know if I can be bothered with the aggravation.'

'They're no match for us lot. We'll walk it, Ethan. Don't you worry your pretty little head about it.'

Ethan replaced his cap, his initials 'ET' carelessly inked into the school shield, and put his arm around Holly. 'As always, you are my number one fan.'

She unravelled herself and gave him a friendly slap.

'Holly, these girls will have vocal training, singing lessons, whatever they ask Mummy Dearest for–we'll be up against a troop of starlets. Just you wait.'

'Do I look worried?' Holly asked, her face set in full mock-shock. 'You do stress over the maddest stuff, Ethe. Just relax. We'll get through it.'

Ethan walked in silence, his jaw set stern, kicking new biker boots all the way.

'Like your new boots.'

'Thanks, Holly. I nicked them from Dave's wardrobe. He never wears them. Lazy oaf – rotten to the core. He never leaves the house.'

'Is he still knocking your mum about? She should get out, you know. He's scary.'

'He doesn't scare me. And he's too drunk these days to do too much damage. And I don't stress. Okay?'

'Okay,' she smiled, stepping aside for Ethan to enter through the heavy wooden doors.

This year, she just knew the game plans and the politics of being top of the school. This year, she was prepared. And to be forewarned was always to be forearmed. Her mum always told her that.

The corridor was busy; bodies pushing along left or right, with Holly and Ethan unsure where to go. Holly headed towards the hall, where the school plans would be set up for the bemused and confused to check where they should be.

'Are you coming?' she called, as Ethan was still standing statuesque in the middle of the corridor.

'I'm with you!' he yelled, reaching out and grabbing her arm in mock rescue, before they joined the rabble of bodies up the staircase and towards the hall.

## Chapter 8

# Holly

'COME ON EVERYONE, file in. Find a chair and sit down. No, I don't want you loitering at the back, Joseph, I'm right over here and I do not want to lose my voice on the first day back at school.'

'Grab us a seat Holly, I'll be right there.'

Holly took her seat on the third and back row of a small semi-circle of carefully placed wooden chairs, their once polished sheen now scratched and etched to reveal many hues of the light brown wood. Mr Hopkins sat on the stage facing them, his black shiny brogues tapping rhythm as they all took their places.

The students filed in noisily, chairs scraping and clattering as they took their seats. A small group of girls–their hair identically pin-curled with faces betraying slight smudges of mascara and rouge, lipstick lightly placed to evoke a little colour. Anything more and they'd be sure to be collected by the school nurse to wash their painted faces with cobalt soap. Tittering and twittering, they took their places on the front row, adjusting their hair and watching for any undue attention from the classmates they looked down upon.

'Right class, if I can have your attention everyone . . .'

'Okay class. I'm calling all members of the drama group. Anyone still talking can go now.'

That shut them up.

This wasn't class, this was lunchtime drama group and there were different expectations here. You only came if you wanted to be involved either on or off stage. Time wasted affected the whole performance, the rehearsal time, the actual run and everything in between. If Mr Hopkins did not think the production was up to it, he always pulled it after the dress rehearsal to the lower school. This had last happened before his Ethan or Holly's time, but the reality that Mr Hopkins always kept to his threats, kept the drama group on their toes and eager to please.

'The production we're going to be working towards is *Oliver Twist*, with our own student take on it of course. Hands up if you've seen the play. Holly, Ethan, Mollie—okay. First things first, I need you all to read it before the end of the half term. I have copies of the novel which you can borrow, should your families be yet to discover the delights of Dickens; but anyone who can purchase their own copies would be doing themselves and their families a real favour. Treat yourselves to a film verion of it - the David Lean version would be a good place to start. Yes, Poppy, it is a black and white film but it won't kill you. It might even educate you a little and will certainly give insight into the darker elements we'll be playing with in our version.'

'Fagin is a child snatcher, a thief, and a wanted criminal. The kids like him because they have a roof over their heads and he doesn't beat them. In fact, he keeps them from the workhouse; so in the boys' eyes, he is a veritable Father Christmas.'

Holly smiled. It was good to be back here.

'Sir, sir! Who will be playing Nancy? I have had singing lessons over the holiday and my dad feels I now have the voice worthy of a lead part.' Clementine Banks flicked her dark hair back over one shoulder with her final words, as a flourish.

Holly and Ethan sighed in unison before sneaking a smile at each other.

36

Mr Hopkins was unshaken. 'Auditions in two weeks. Every student will be asked to choose a monologue from the script and a song from the musical. Everyone will have their moment to shine, Clementine.'

Clementine's dad may well have been Chair of Governors, with half the money earned in this town from his betting shops; yet to Mr Hopkins, Clementine was just another student. Holly liked that about him. Most teachers quaked in their boots, should Clementine drop a cushioned threat in to the equation, but for Mr Hopkins, it was all about the talent.

'Okay, folks. Time to go. The bell's about to go off for afternoon lessons. Next week, we'll meet up and spend time on audition pieces, so please come prepared. Off you go!'

The room erupted in to lively chatter. Chairs clattered and scraped on wooden floors as the students left in a swarming mass of bodies.

'What you gonna do, Holly?'

'Not sure yet, Ethan. I might read through the script tonight. Why don't you come back after school?'

'Nothing to rush home for,' he shrugged.

'Oh, wait! We'll have to pick my brothers up on the way, they started school today. The infant school looks tiny now, wait 'til you see it.'

'Does it still smell of witch hazel and furniture polish?'

Holly laughed. 'Just like it always did. Do you remember the Green Wellies Brigade?'

'Mr Bartholomew was a strange old thing, wasn't he?'

'Eccentric, I think we'd call it these days. I thought he was lovely— he always had time for us.'

'And those gardens . . . how amazing were they? I'm amazed how we ever learned anything else, we were always there fixing the weeds, pruning, and planting.'

'Do you remember when Becky ran down the field to the gates that day though? He could be a bit scary.'

'I'd forgotten about that. He really frightened her—and us! Never step beyond the Healing Garden. A rule is a rule, never to be broken!'

'Those woods are full of people walking dogs though. He was only trying to keep us safe.'

'Well, I've never seen anyone in there.'

'Ethan, when have you been down there?

'Only for a dare last year. It's just overgrown woods. I didn't see anyone.'

'Did you go in?'

'You can't get in—the gate's locked and it's too high to climb up. I just looked through the gates. No big deal really.'

'Isn't it funny what you're scared of when you're little?' Holly smiled. 'I thought we'd get eaten alive by dangerous dogs foaming at the mouth if we ventured anywhere near! He scared me half to death that day.'

'It did the trick though, didn't it? We never went down there.'

'Well you did, you idiot. Lucky there were no wild dogs there that day.'

'It was just a daft story, Holly—just to keep us from wandering away from school grounds. Nothing more.'

'Whatever you say. Are you coming after school with me then?'

'Fine by me. Any chance of tea round at yours?'

'Of course. It goes without saying,' Holly laughed. Mum no longer asked Ethan if he was staying for tea when he arrived home with Holly after school. It came with the territory. They knew that it might be all Ethan got for supper and they always managed to feed him up before sending him home.

'Thanks, Hol.'

'Are you thinking of what mum's cooked already?! I can see it in your eyes!'

'Well, she might have done a roast dinner—I can always dream,' he grinned.

'Not on a Monday night. It's more likely to be Sunday's leftovers, but you'll get what you're given, Ethan Thomas!'

'Did you get me a script? I forgot to pick one up!' he started, turning back.

Waving a second copy in front of his eyes, she smiled. 'We can read through these tonight and get some idea about who we might like to be.'

'Great. Thanks, Hol,' Ethan grinned again. He was pretty hopeless. But he was her best friend and she had his back. Someone had to.

'I'd be happy enough as one of Fagin's boys,' Ethan grinned.

'Me, too,' Holly sighed. 'If the artful Dodger is taken, I'd do anything!' she sang.

With that, they linked arms and disappeared through the wooden double doors to afternoon registration.

## CHAPTER 9

# Holly

SCHOOL OVER, THE two rushed to pick up the boys after their first day at school. They were full of news after their first day.

'We played football at playtime and our team won!'

'We had sausage and mash for dinner—with gravy!'

'Miss Thompson says that we have to read our reading books tonight.'

'–and you have to hear me read, Holly. Can you hear me read?'

'And me, Holly. Will you hear me read too?'

After bribing the twins with a half bag of fruit gums, the group wandered down to the conservation area, where the Green Wellington brigade had spent their lunchtimes all those years before.

'It's hardly changed at all!' Holly laughed as they took in the rows of plants neatly planted and the old wooden wheel placed in its centre, with herbs carefully planted along each of its spokes. Holly ran her hand through the river of lavender bordering one side, releasing the floral scent, as pungent as ever.

Blue bells and forget-me-nots mingled with rosemary and thyme as they trod carefully along the path, delicate as always.

'It's still as I remember it,' Holly whispered.

'Didn't Old Bartholomew say it had to stay like this? I remember he told us all that the garden would be maintained like this as a sanctuary for future students, something like that. Bit precious, if you ask me.'

'It's his legacy though, Ethan. I think it's rather lovely that they've kept it like this. I wonder how they've kept it so similar. Look, even the daisies along the bottom wall are the same.'

'It'll all be written down somewhere, if I remember Bartholomew. Don't you remember the big, old book he carried everywhere with him, like something out of Victorian school days? All he needed was a black schoolmaster's cloak and he'd have looked the part!'

'Well, I quite liked him,' Holly defended. 'He always reminded me of something out of Sherlock Holmes–all that brown clothing. Tweed and corduroy to the death.'

'Did he die?'

'No, he's still here, he's pretty ancient now though.'

The scent of wild flowers, sweet yet dusty, hit them as they walked closer.

'Can you remember these plant names? He used to always be telling us–'

'I don't think I'd be able to now. There might be a few of those wooden stakes he wrote on hidden away.'

On their hands and knees, they steadily worked their way along the rows, calling out any they found or remembered.

'Dusty Millers–'

'Evening Primrose–'

'Jasmine–'

'This is the butterfly bush. Do you remember how full it used to get of butterflies in the summer?'

Holly sat by an old wooden wagon wheel placed flat on the ground, its faded weathered spokes separating the herbs from each other.

'I think this was my favourite,' Ethan told the boys who had run over to take a closer look. 'Can you see how the herbs' names have been written on the wheel? Camphor, Juniper, Moonwort, Pennyroyal, Rosemary, Sage, Silver Thyme, Sleep Wort–one for each of the spokes. Smells amazing.'

Jake rubbed his finger and thumb on the silky sage leaf and took a deep sniff. 'Smells like stuffing!' he smiled, licking his fingers. 'Urrggh!'

Tom pulled an equally horrified face and took a deep breath. 'That tickles my nose!'

The boys ran off again, back and forth through a nearby bramble arch studded with a pale blue roses, as they continued on their way along.

'Blue moon roses–'

'Oh yes. I'd forgotten when we planted those. Do you remember how scratched Mr B got weaving that up there?'

'They look pretty though. I didn't believe they'd bloom blue. Do you remember how he was always planting blue flowers? His favourite colour or something.'

'To keep us safe and sound. Funny old thing. I still love those blooms. They still look special after all this time.'

'It's our secret garden, Holly!' Tom laughed, hugging his sister before running away again. 'Let's not tell anyone!'

Ethan and Holly smiled. 'I always felt like that, Ethan. You know?'

'It just kept me close to our Bette, that's why I came. It was the last place she came to before–'

Ethan shook his head and waited for the boys to come close again. 'Hey listen, you two. This is a special place for anyone who wants to come here. It's the Healing Garden, a special place for the school. Me and your sister helped plant some of this when we were here.'

'Really?' Tom frowned. 'Was that a hundred years ago?'

'I think the garden started ages ago –my big sister was here ten years ago and she helped with it too.'

'I didn't know you had a big sister, Ethan,' Jake started. Holly pushed him and shook her head.

Ethan started back to school. 'Best get back, Hol. Before your mum worries.'

'What?' Jake shouted. 'What did I do?'

'Nothing,' Holly sighed. 'Let's go.'

The four trooped back up the hill to the school yard in silence.

The twins chattered on the way home, their conversations weaving over each other all the way to their blue front door.

'Can we play outside, Holly?'

'Can we, Holly? Can we go play football?'

'Yes, yes, yes! My ears are ringing!'

Keys turned, the boys were through the door and out the back in seconds.

'Are they going to be like this every day?' Ethan moaned. 'I don't know if I can cope!'

'You don't have to come home with me, Ethan. I don't want to put you to any trouble!'

Ethan was so often at the house, Holly's mum had started making extra to accommodate him as a matter of course last year. Holly only hoped she had predicted Ethan's un-invited presence when preparing the evening meal.

'Hi, Mum!' Holly called as she closed the front door and kicked off her boots.

'Hello, darling! How was it?'

'Fine'

'What were you up to today?'

'Stuff.'

'Alright, Mrs Dawson?' Ethan threw his bag down in the doorway and sat down.

'Drink?'

'Water, please.'

The three sat at the kitchen table, the silence broken by a thirsty gulping of water and the boys' chatter outside.

'We took the boys to see the school garden,' Ethan confided. 'I don't think anyone would mind, but we just sneaked down after school. It's just the same as when we were there.'

'They kept it just the same, would you believe that? Even the daisies are by the wall still, and the rows of lavender—still smell the same.'

'Did you know they kept it going? I didn't know that, the boys wanted to show us. It's just as it always was.'

'When Bette – when she disappeared, they planted more flowers and built the sun dial there. Like in memory of her. I like to think it might help her find her way back to us one day.'

Cara pressed her lips together hard. 'Children aren't allowed down there on their own. You really mustn't go down there.'

'The boys wanted to show us, Mum.'

'They are five years old, hardly the ones you should be listening to. You can be really stupid, Holly, sometimes. I thought you were a little more sensible than that.'

'Mum!'

'You must not do that again. Do you understand? Fancy taking the boys down there without an adult. Anything could have happened!'

'Okay, okay. God!'

'And there's no need to blaspheme either. I don't know what gets in to you, lady. Watch yourself.'

As Holly's mum stormed upstairs, the two looked aghast at each other.

'Wow, Hol. Never heard your mum get that stroppy.'

'Don't know what got in to her.'

'It wasn't even that big a deal. Can't wait to see her face when you really screw up!'

'Thanks, Ethan.'

'That's what friends are for. Can I have some toast or something? She'll be ages now you've upset her.' He winked. 'I'm starving.'

'I'll talk to her later.' Holly exhaled slowly to release the tightening in her chest. 'Do you want jam with that?'

'Go on then.'

'You know where the bread is, and jam's in the fridge. What did your last servant die of?'

Ethan helped himself, popping two slices of bread in the battered old silver toaster. 'Disobedience, Hol,' he winked. So watch it.'

The two boys ran in, zooming Lego aeroplanes around their heads.

'Did your sister really plant one of the gardens at school?' Jake started.

'Jake–'

'What? He told us she did.'

Ethan rubbed a hand heavily across his forehead. 'Yes, that's right.'

'Toilet time, Jake', Holly sang brightly, 'quick!'

'But I don't need to–'

Holly had Jake up the stairs and in the toilet before he had time to finish his sentence.

'Ow, Holly!'

'Just shut up and listen for a minute will you?'

'You hurt me.'

'No, I didn't. Now listen here–Ethan's sister disappeared. He's not seen her since he was a baby, so it's hard for him to talk about it.'

'Well, I didn't know.'

'And you do now. So go and have your tinkle.'

Holly shut the bathroom door and waited while Jake crashed about.

As the table was cleared, Jake eyed Ethan with blushing cheeks and a tightly pressed mouth.

'I might go, Hol,' Ethan mouthed.

Holly followed him from the table.

'You don't have to, Ethan,' whispered Holly as they stood alone in the hallway.

'It's just weird when people talk about Bette like that. I forget she's gone most of the time. I can hardly remember her but then sometimes I remember little glimmers of her like when I smell roses – she always wore rose perfume of my mum's. It's like she's with me.'

Holly rubbed his arm. 'Don't mind him, Ethan. He's just being curious. Come back inside. You've not had your toast.'

'You're alright. Best get back to the madhouse. See what's kicking off there. I'll be glad when I'm gone.'

'Don't worry, Ethe, we'll be sharing a sweaty student house before you know it. We'll be in college and you'll be away from it all.'

'Can't wait that long, Hol. Mum's a mess and my step dad's an idiot.'

'You can always stay at mine.'

'Dunno. Might take you up on that soon.'

As he strode purposefully back home, Holly wished she could run after him. But she couldn't change his past for him; poor thing, and she certainly couldn't change his present.

## CHAPTER 10

# Cara

HER DREAMS HAD been filled once more with the baby. *Walking along the castle wall, steadily down the grassy dugout that once held water and the corpses of valiant knights and unlucky horses. Deep into the trenches where wild hedgerows now grew. A muffled call or squeal rings out. Sounds like laughter or breaking glass. Running towards the sound, her long skirts tangling round her. Seeing the baby, wrapped in white muslin; a tiny hand protruding forward reaching out to her. Scratching itself on the low-lying holly bush and calling out to her in a tiny yet compelling voice, 'Find me, Cara. Here I am.'*

And now the dreams were every night, where once they were only once or twice a week. They stayed with her during the day too–the baby's arm too near the thorny branches, setting her teeth on edge as the memory replayed in her mind's eye.

*And always under an inky sky, studded with white stars. The milk spill of a full moon casting its reflected light across the deep red berries that frame this small child.*

As Cara reached out for her, this tiny girl child, the dreams would spiral away, bringing her back in to the present, her body tangled up in her bedclothes and tense from her attempts to pull the child with her from her dreams.

Cara remembered a particularly difficult morning, some years before, a few years after she had found Holly and was working at the local school. She was sleeping less and less, yet when she did, her dreams were filled with babies and trenches and rain and moonshine. She barely knew what day it was most mornings, waking up to half written plans and half-baked lessons delivered in a trance while her head was elsewhere.

'Are you fit to be in school?' asked Mr Bartholomew, concerned rather than chastising; she knew that, but his words still scratched at her and she flinched.

'Come and have a drink of sweet tea. It does wonders for the nerves.'

Cara nodded and took a seat in the beige-and-orange staffroom, high backed chairs in a semi-circle around a low coffee table patterned with rings made by sticky cups over the years.

The staffroom was otherwise empty; a shell of file laden bookcases and tatty furniture, staff making preparations for the day in their rooms by now.

Cara leaned forward in her chair and stretched her arms out in front of her, unlocking the tight muscles in her shoulders. 'I'm just tired, Henry. Trying to keep it all together but just a bit behind. Nothing I can't fix.'

'Are you sleeping, Miss Evans?'

'Cara, please.' She smiled at his formalities, perhaps in his late forties, yet could be so much older or perhaps even younger. 'Not very well. But I'm just busy with my friend and work – you know how it is. I mustn't grumble.'

She sipped the sweet treacle of the tea, thick and syrupy yet stronger than her usual cup. Just sitting here was helpful and she smiled at her colleague. 'Thank you, Henry. I needed that little pit stop. But I must be getting back.'

'How is Sally doing these days?'

'I forgot you used to work with Sally, didn't you? Was she here on a teaching placement?'

'I saw her with Bette last week, and the new little one. Ethan, is it?'

Cara nodded. 'I'm not sure how well she's doing really,' Cara lied. 'She keeps to herself.'

Henry nodded again and wandered over to the sink area just beyond them. 'Send her my regards, Miss Evans.' He carefully washed and dried the two cups regimentally. 'She seems just a little fragile at present. We would do well to keep a close eye on her and an even closer eye on those children of hers.'

'I'll do my best.'

'I've spoken to a Miss Trench from the authorities about the family, Cara, just so that you are aware. I have concerns about the children and of course, about poor Sally; but those children are our priority. She has been supporting the family since Bette was born, I'm not sure if Sally mentioned it, and those children are not getting the best shot at life.'

'She's just ill, Henry. This Miss Trench has been snooping around that family for years. If there was really something, they would have acted by now.'

'She's just not coping. And the drinking is not helping. Let's try to be honest here. You are doing a lot more than you are letting on. Agreed?'

'I'm just being a good friend, Henry. She has a very difficult time with that husband of hers. Let's try to support her and not take the kids off her.'

'Cara, really. That's for Miss Trench to investigate now. Let's not jump to any rash decisions. We need to look at how the children are looked after. Step away so we can make sure she can cope on her own.'

Cara had made her excuses and left as quickly as she could. Sally had never looked after those children and she would lose them if she wasn't careful, Cara knew that. There was a certain irony in the fact that Sally had had two children without any trouble, and then lost her way while Cara had only her dreams of her one day baby. She found some comfort in these and the thought that a child may one day be hers.

## CHAPTER 11

# Holly

*I*T WAS ALMOST *as if the earth beneath her feet was coming alive with every step, transforming with the upward pull of her bare toes into a living entity.*

*Below the translucent soil, roots glowed neon, a cornflower yellow, pulsating in time with every step she made. It was as if the whole woodland was breathing with her. Throbbing roots stretched away from her feet, entwining together to light up the area around her, gently coaxing her farther and farther in to the garden, away from the wrought iron gates she had pushed open some moments earlier. Entering this unknown place in silence away from the world she knew.*

*With every root shining gently through the soil, a neighbouring plant would shudder gently, its mossy greenness gilded momentarily as it stretched upwards before bowing back into itself and fading.*

*Glossy ferns unfurled to greet her as she tiptoed over the soil glistening dewy fronds, before retreating back tightly curled as she passed.*

*Her footsteps led their own rhythm, the garden alive around her pulsating an accompanying beat to the music in her head.*

*The night sky rolled above her - diamonds in velvet, sparkling and twinkling against the midnight hue.*

*Her head felt suddenly full and heavy, dizzy and distorted, as the earth and heavens rolled around her. Falling, she reached forward to grab handfuls of loose moss against the roots of a small gnarled tree. She sat.*

*The world pulsed a very different rhythm now: more urgency, desperation, force, faster and faster until Holly could bear it no longer. Curling up against the rough bark of the tree, she closed her eyes and covered her ears with her hands, shaking her head, shaking the sounds and the chaos out of her.*

*Silence.*

*The quiet cry of a baby sounded out against the enormity of quiet all around. Holly opened her eyes in to absolute nothingness—black, clean, silent, nothing.*

*Another cry could be heard in the distance. And another. And another. And another, until a gentle chorus of needy harmonic cries called out, not in distress as such, more in need of an answer.*

*'Hello?' she called. 'Hello?'*

*The crying continued.*

*'Who is there? This is madness. Who is there?' she called again.*

*A tinkling sound, as delicate as a waterfall, rang out. Holly had heard that sound before. Gentler than a breaking champagne glass, yet harsh at the edges. A laugh.*

*'Hello?'*

*Tinkling rang out, surrounding her like a whirlwind around her, and she knew.*

*The ground around her feet felt harder, uneven, and unrelenting beneath her feet.*

*Looking down, she saw to her horror: she was sitting on the writhing, crying bodies of the babies she had heard earlier.*

*'No!' Holly jumped away from the mound, away from the figures as they moved once more, and then stopped.*

*The babies were still and Holly feared for a moment her weight had killed them all. How many lay here? Their naked bodies were the colour of the soil—dirty, dull like clay. She counted nine, as they lay motionless, as if film was paused on a screen.*

*The babies were clay. Tentatively, she rubbed her first finger across the cheek of one and it moved slightly towards her, its face nuzzling towards her hand.*

*'Oh!'*

*The tinkling again. The laughter again.*

*'I know I'm dreaming! I know this isn't real, please tell me what's going on!'*

*A voice rang out–a melodic glass chime type of a sound–yet she could hear every word . . .*

*'One decade past, a child is lost*
*For faerie lore decrees*
*A changeling lives a decade long*
*Once the human child is seized.*

*They live a whispered half life*
*Once human babes are gone*
*Two lives we take, your freedom to make*
*The moon child will live on.'*

Holly shook her head slowly. The words hung around her–a blend of mist and spider webs seemed wrapped around her. She could barely breathe.

'No! No! No!' she shouted, pushing against the tight binding, her arms flexing, her legs kicking.

'It's okay, it's okay! Holly, Holly! It's just a dream, my darling–a dream. Wake up, my love, and wake up now.'

Holly opened her eyes. Her mum sat over her, her hands gripping Holly's arms tightly.

'Mum, Mum–I was dreaming. I'm so sorry.'

She realised her face was wet through and her hair lay across her cheeks wet with perspiration.

Mum smiled. 'That must have been some dream, darling! You were shouting, kicking, punching . . . You were all wrapped up in your duvet cover. No wonder you're wet through. Do you want a glass of water?'

'I'll get it, Mum.'

'No, let me. I can do it.'

Holly sat up in bed and switched on her bedside light and pulled the wet strands of chestnut hair off her face.

What was that all about?

Holly could remember every element of that dream, frozen in a series of frames across her brain. Some sort of charm or spell, it sounded like, just before she woke up; and the clay babies under her feet–it was macabre and disturbing, yet somehow, from somewhere deep inside, it seemed to make sense.

Her Mum came back in. 'Here you go, petal, then try and get some sleep.'

'What's a changeling?'

Her mum's face set. 'Why?'

'I heard the word somewhere–

*A changeling lives a decade long*
*Once the human child is seized.*

What does that even mean? Is it a poem or a story or something?'

'Is that what your dream was about?'

'I don't know. And they're babies, aren't they?

*Two lives we take, your freedom to make*
*The moon child will live on.'*

'Stop that, Holly! What on earth did you eat before bedtime? You can't have heard that, you were mistaken.'

'Have you heard that before? Two lives we take, whispered half-lives, to make a moonchild? That sounds really freaky, Mum. I'm scared.'

'There is nothing to be scared of, Holly. I've made sure of it. You are safe in this village. Do not worry.'

'I'm having these awful dreams. Babies who are like clay or pot or something like that, and I'm on top of them. They're scary, Mum. I don't want to sleep if I dream that again.'

'Holly, things always seem worse in the middle of the night. It's just a dream. Lay your head down now and just try to get some sleep. School tomorrow.'

'What is a changeling? I've heard it before somewhere.'

'Night, night, Holly,' her Mum whispered. 'We're not doing this now. Do your research in the morning.'

Holly tightened the blanket around her as her Mum turned out the light and smiled up into the darkness. 'It was really strange, Mum. I think my dream was trying to tell me something.'

'Goodnight, Holly, you silly thing. You read far too many fairy stories. Eyes closed and sweet dreams.'

Cara was thankful for the darkness, her eyes hot with tears. Ten years had passed and she was scared of what the next few months would bring. She knew what must pass, but wasn't sure how she would cope, knowing she would have to stand by and let it all happen once more. Holly was the most precious child, her wished-for child, and had to be protected at all costs. But were it to be yet another child from the village, Cara wasn't sure if her nerves would stand it.

## CHAPTER 12

# Ethan

'HELLO, MRS DAVIS!' Ethan shouted into the darkness of the corridor.

A muted voice called out greetings from the kitchen. 'I thought you might pop by. I've made plenty!'

Holly smiled to herself. Mum allowed herself so often to be the shelter in the storm. Even when life was perhaps not at its best for her, she always had time for others.

Ethan smiled. 'She's great, your mum. I'm starving.'

The table was hurriedly rearranged and set for five places before the four noisily went about taking their seats – mum placing dishes of steaming sausages, mash and various vegetables in the centre.

'Help yourselves to more, kids. There's plenty more to go round.'

'You've put sweet corn on my plate, Mum!'

'Just try it. You might like it, Tom,' Mum replied calmly.

Tom's nose was screwed up tightly, his jaw equally fixed.

'When I was your age, I didn't know what sweet corn was,' Ethan confided in a wide-eyed Tom and Jack. 'All we had at home was take-aways, and beans on toast.'

'Sounds perfect to me!' groaned Jack as he pushed the peas and sweet corn in to separate piles on his plate.

'Not when you have it every night.'

Holly ate in silence. She knew what he was saying. Eating at his house was the exception rather than the rule.

'How is your mum doing, Ethan? I must pop by for a catch up.'

'She's fine, thank you,' he replied curtly. Conversation closed.

'So Mum, have you heard of something called a changeling?'

Holly's mum shook her head. 'Not sure, my love.'

'A what?'

'My nightmare last night: it was something someone said–not sure who–it just stuck with me.'

'You still writing it all down?' Ethan asked.

Holly glanced nervously at Mum. 'Mostly.'

Cara sighed. 'It's a word from Victorian folklore, maybe earlier. Fairies, magic, wizards, and witches, things that go bump in the night. You'll be dragging up stories I told you when you were tiny, that's all!'

'I might look it up, sounds strange . . . was it to do with babies? I keep dreaming about babies too.'

'You could write a story. Miss Green said we've got to write stories next term, so save it all up 'til then. You can write mine for me as well if you like!'

'Whatever, Holly,' she sighed. 'You do whatever you have to do. Dreams are just echoes of something lost, a memory, or a thought– that's all. Try not to worry.'

But Cara knew this was far from true. From a young age, she had too been haunted by dreams. All those years ago, before Holly, before adulthood even, her dreams were filled with stories.

. . . There was always a cost.

## CHAPTER 13
# Holly & Ethan

AFTER TEA, INHALED within minutes, Holly and Ethan found themselves sitting at an empty table.

'Shall we go up to my room?'

'If you like—unless you want to come over to the caves with me.'

'What for?'

'It doesn't matter. I want to check on the drawings again. I've found so many, I reckon there might be more if I go in a little deeper. It's much quieter at night. Do you want to come?'

Holly shook her head. 'I can't come out at night, Ethan. It's one of mum's many rules.' As soon as the words were out of her mouth, she regretted them.

'Yeah. Well, I don't have that trouble.'

'Sorry, Ethe.'

'Don't be.'

'Are you sure it's safe? I don't like the thought of you being out there on your own in the dark. You're just asking for a broken neck!'

They were more like brother and sister these days, with Ethan just relieved to be out of the way of whatever life went on back at his place.

'Tell you what, Hol. If I break my neck, I'll not come running to you for sympathy. How about that?'

She pushed him up the stairs as they ran and he mock-fell on to the landing. 'Ah! My neck!'

'You are losing it, Ethan. You really are.'

Holly's room was almost as she'd left it that morning, although mum had placed a small vase of purple hyacinths on her bedside table that morning to 'brighten up the room and keep the nightmares away'. Holly smiled at the thought of it. Flowers to guard against the night spirits, the stuff of folklore and earth magic, no doubt.

Grabbing the crumpled covers, Holly hastily rearranged her unmade bed, smoothing the top covers before jumping on it and tipping out two copies of rolled up scripts out from her bag.

'Holly—look at them!' Ethan groaned, the curled, tatty pages betraying her clumsiness.

'So-rry!' she sang, a lop-sided grin masking her embarrassment. The neat stacks of stapled papers were no longer as fresh and as new as at lunchtime. She bit her bottom lip to stifle another apology.

'Sir, my dad is paying a fortune for singing lessons so make me a star or he'll have your head!' Ethan dramatized in a high falsetto tone, all flailing arms and fluttering eyelashes. She was forgiven.

Holly fell back on the bed, laughing. 'You're a natural darling. It's a life on the stage for you!' she squawked.

'So who do you want to be?' she asked, determined to get the caves out of Ethan's head and desperate to practise. 'We have as good a chance as anyone there.'

Ethan shrugged. 'Don't mind really. I could do a mean Bill Sykes. I've lived with him long enough. I'll ask for his name to be changed to Idiot Dave, much more fitting.'

Her heart sank. But she knew better than to dwell on it. Ethan wasn't one for sharing his home troubles. 'So you have read the script!' she smiled.

'No, but I've seen it far too many times—creakily black and white, and the musical too many times to count. It's mum's favourite Christmas film. I reckon she sees herself as a bit of a Nancy.'

His poor mum. A mess now, but Holly's mum knew her way back when they were at school together before her life took a nose dive. She had been clever, pretty, but easily led, falling for his dad and leaving school with something rather more than the usual exam results.

'Ooh, Nancy. I bet our starlets have got their hearts set on that. There's going to be a few cat fights over that part, I reckon!'

He smiled. 'Do you really want to do this tonight?'

'I'm not going down to the woods, Ethe. Mum won't let me.'

'She doesn't have to know.'

Holly's eyebrows arched, her mouth twisted sideways.

'Okay, slave driver. I'll be Mr Bumble and you can be the lovely Mrs Bumble. We'll make a great double act.'

'That we do,' she smiled. 'Maybe we should go at the weekend instead, Ethan—it gets dark quickly and you don't want to be stuck in a cave after sunset.'

'That's what torches are for, scaredy-cat. Just meet me tomorrow after school and we'll get there on the first bus, we can rehearse on the way. Win-win if you ask me!'

Holly knew in her heart this was a bad idea. 'Why tomorrow?'

He answered in his stock horror voice, dripping with Count Dracula. 'Before the nights draw in and we are doomed to 4 pm twilights, my dear.'

'You're impossible,' she sighed, shaking her head. 'You're not going on your own. There's something I have to do first, but don't go without me. I'll be as quick as I can.'

CHAPTER 14

# Holly

THE LIBRARY, ALL dusty pages and polished tables, was hers that evening. She had half an hour before meeting Ethan, and Holly knew she had a limited time to grab the books she needed.

Folklore and English literature were her favourite sections of the library, and she hurried to the corner where a leather chair and old oak table waited for her. Seven books, carefully selected after poring through the index pages, piled up invitingly and Holly was cross she's left herself such little time to do this.

'You are being a busy little bee,' a light voice whispered behind her.

'Oh, hello Miss Sharp! You made me jump.'

'These books are a little dusty. You'll be getting me in to trouble,' she smiled, wiping the battered leather covers clean. 'An interesting selection here. Cara's daughter, isn't it?'

'Yes, Holly.'

'Of course. The holly baby.'

Holly frowned and shook her head.

'What are you looking for?'

Holly covered her notes and sat down hard in her chair. 'I'm just doing some research.'

'For a school project? Or a personal quest?'

'I'm in a bit of a rush, Miss Sharp, I can't stay long. Did you once work with mum then?'

'Before you were born, my lovely. Is there anything here I can help you with? What I don't know about faerie folk could be written on the back of a postage stamp.'

'Changelings,' Holly smiled. 'I've had a dream—well, lots of them actually—and in it someone calls a baby a changeling. I just want to find out what they are.'

'Does your mum know you're concerned about this?'

'I'm not overly concerned,' Holly lied. Her pinking cheeks betrayed her. 'I don't think mum knows what they are. I just want to find out, that's all.'

'Well,' Miss Sharp smiled, 'they do say that knowledge is power and I feel it would help if you knew what your dreams were trying to tell you.'

'They're just dreams, Miss Sharp. Mum reckons I've just watched something on the TV or read something, and my subconscious is just processing it.'

'Really, Holly?' Miss Sharp picked up the first of the books and blew a stubborn cobweb from the top corner of the binding. 'And is that what you believe?'

'Not really. Mum is just a bit practical. She doesn't seem to see things the way I see them.'

'That's to be expected. Your mum has closed her mind to that which she finds painful. You must forgive her for that. Her life has been a difficult one, shrouded with much pain and torment. You look surprised. You really should ask her to be honest with you.'

'How do you know my mum so well?'

'Come. Let's tackle this personal project of yours. Is there anywhere else you need to be?'

'Soon. I'm meeting someone after school.'

'We should hurry then—the nights are drawing in once more.' Miss Sharp positioned the table lamp a little closer to them and clicked it on under the lampshade. The table flooded with yellow lamplight, sharpening the words on the page and spotlighting their quest a little.

Scribbling frantically, Holly found one page dedicated to changelings in the index and turned the pages of the first red book:

*In European folklore, a changeling is an irregular, rejected offspring of dwarves, elves, or faeries sneakily substituted by them for a human child. A human child is then raised instead to strengthen the faerie population, while the changeling dies on the dawn of its adolescence to spawn a new and healthy faerie.*

Holly frowned. 'That's horrible,' she gasped.

'Oh, but they are,' Miss Sharp mused. 'Terrible creatures. And not so much a folktale either,' she whispered, nodding her head as Holly's eyes grew wide. 'You would be surprised.'

'So how would that even work?'

Miss Sharp adjusted her hands in her lap and leaned forward, her green eyes dancing in the lamplight.

She read from the page:

*Two human children, neglected by their own parents, must be taken over one decade to feed two faerie babies–a* **changeling** *then replaces each human baby and grows up in his/her place dying a decade later. This act often occurs in payment for a human wish made to faeries, fulfilling the prophecy of two half-lives to create the moonchild's life on Earth. These stolen babies were deemed to be unwanted children by the faerie folk and so were removed to serve faeries. The changelings, before adolescence, die after serving the changeling their charmed blood thirty days after feeding a new fairy child.*

'That would be terrible,' Holly whispered. 'And you believe in this stuff?'

'Many years ago, faeries ruled a kingdom, their own beyond our world.' Miss Sharp spoke in barely a whisper.

'In folk lore . . .' Holly interrupted.

'Some say . . .' Miss Sharp continued, 'that faeries once ruled their kingdom and the other magical folk within it. Over time, their magic waned and their fights for supremacy started to be lost to other groups. The faeries were losing their power. The woodlands were once more safe places to go, and humans were no longer fearful of the shadows as once they were.'

'So the stories said that they had to use darker magic to regain power?'

Miss Sharp pointed at the page once more. 'Folklore tells us about a time when faeries discovered the power of human blood–the younger the better–and looked for a way to harness this power to their own advantage.'

Holly closed the book, crossing her arms over to it and meeting Miss Sharp's gaze. 'You know more than these books can tell me, Miss Sharp. I've got to go and meet a friend, but I would like to talk to you again, if that's ok?'

'Of course, my dear. You must hurry though. You may miss him.'

Holly frowned. 'Who?'

'Go quickly–he has quite the hot head and he'll go without you.'

Holly shook her head and collected her belongings, stuffing them in to her satchel. 'You're right. I don't' know how you know, but you are right. I'd better run.'

'Come tomorrow after school, Holly. We will continue.'

'Thank you, Miss Sharp. I'll see you again tomorrow!'

## CHAPTER 15

# Ethan

UMBRELLAS PITCHED AGAINST the sky, their shields of black, red, blue and a thousand more, students hurried on their way home through the rainy assault.

Ethan pulled up his coat collar and walked against the torrential downpour, his boots kicking out against the watery pathway to a bus shelter just off the main school road.

Holly should be here, he scowled, sitting wet and shivery while the bus made its way to him.

He knew he really shouldn't be going tonight, but he had waited three nights for Holly to agree to the visit. Now, as she had let him down in his hour of need, he could wait no longer. He rarely stayed away as long, the pull of the place being so strong, the secrets of the caves luring him there. He knew this was madness, but maybe the rain would stop soon and within three hours he'd be walking home in the dusky night, his head filled with the cave's secrets once more.

The bus rumbled its way along the Pennine road, jolting him sharply against the glass window. His wet coat sticking to him, his trousers rubbing under his knees and around his waistband. Gentle, persistent rain continued against the bus window, blurring the world outside to nothing more than streaks of greys and blues as he watched the village disappear out of sight.

'Good afternoon, Ethan,' an old voice called from behind him. He turned slowly to see the local shopkeeper, Mr Khan, smiling at him from three seats back.

'Hello, Mr Khan.'

'I don't much like this rain, son.'

'No, me neither.'

'Looks like you'll catch a cold, boy,' he continued.

Ethan smiled and turned back to his window.

'How's Mrs Davies keeping?'

He coloured. 'Fine,' he lied, knowing the shopkeeper only saw his mum when she stumbled in for an extra bottle of spirits while Ethan was at school. Everyone knew. But they still served her.

'Good, good.'

Ethan turned away from the old busybody. It didn't do to talk to the shopkeeper as anything you said was passed around the village like a bad game of Chinese whispers, only to get back to him five times harsher and ten times further away from the truth.

'And what would you be doing out on your own at this time of the afternoon, sir?' the old man continued, to the back of Ethan's head. 'This is not your usual way home now, is it?'

Ethan pretended not to hear. He wished he'd brought a book or something, anything to avoid the mindless chitchat of these nosy neighbours.

'Visiting friends, perhaps? A girlfriend?'

Ethan turned round sharply. 'My aunt and uncle live along here. I'm visiting them for tea.'

'I see. What a treat.'

'Indeed.' Ethan turned back and opened his bag, remembering a battered copy of Oliver Twist he'd thankfully borrowed from the school library. He waved it above his head. 'Homework. Do you mind if I get on?'

'Not at all, not at all. Study maketh the man,' Mr Khan smiled.

'Thank you, sir.' Ethan smiled as kindly as he could muster, then shrank down in his seat.

Now was as good a time as any, he realised, to read the first few chapters before the auditions next week. A good twenty minutes more on a bus with Mr Khan required the company of Oliver Twist firmly between them. God bless Charles Dickens, he smiled. He opened the red leathery front cover and smoothed the thin parchment as he read the first lines . . .

The countryside had opened up beyond the town and the village, the bus now one ambling through grey stony roads and wild hedgerows on either side. Trees stretched over the road sheltering them from the continuing rain, yet here, the raindrops seemed less and the air cleaner.

As Ethan jumped down from the bus, his boots splashed noisily into a deep puddle that had lain undetected until he stood inches under water. 'No!' he shouted, while stepping out from this pothole onto the grassy verge. The bus had gone and his comedy moment had gone unnoticed. For that he was thankful.

Slipping down the muddy bank, Ethan realised that the rain would have to stop soon for him to be able to get back up the slope for later. The rain had eased a little and seemed to have reduced to a gentle drizzle.

Before he knew it, he was sliding down the grassy, muddy hillside, unable to stop himself and unsure how he would ever get out again. The valley came up to meet him before he had even registered this, and he landed on his back at the base of the valley, wet through, mud across his back and legs. His hands were full of wet clay, thick with mud from steering himself down the valley at high speed. In snow, he had moved marginally faster–yet come out a whole lot cleaner–he realised, shaking his wet fringe and showering his face even further. There was a point when you could not get any wetter, on a day like this, and Ethan observed that he had certainly reached that stage. Equally, there was that point when getting muddier was not possible, and he was sure he had reached that stage.

Maybe by sheltering in the caves, he'd get a chance to dry off. Slipping across the grass, he carefully climbed up on to the limestone ridge and sat, glad to be clear of the mud and grass. The wet stone was slippery as ice, yet he perched there precariously for a moment catching his breath.

The caves spread round the valley in a semi-circle like the old caravan of wagons around a campfire, carved in to the yellow stone of the valley above the grass, and mud at the bottom of this basin. A central lake had been forced upon the ice-age structure some years before, at the insistence of a rather passionate Victorian environmentalist who paid for the privilege in a final bid to deter a railway being carved through this fine structure's centre.

And now, the place existed in a timeless void–untouched since then, save for the occasional supporting hoist as the caves' interiors slowly crumbled from extensive fossil hunts and curious explorers. Yet no one, Ethan was sure, no one had ever ventured as deep as his family, who had passed the secret down through the boys of the family, until Ethan's uncle had shared with him this place. This sanctuary he could escape to away from the home life he barely coped with, away from the parents who barely noticed he was gone.

Five caves were visible, yet only two of them were any more than carved dips in the rock, providing little more than shelter from such a storm. However, the third cave offered so much more and was the reason Ethan had spent much of his summer holidays down here.

Beyond the simple carved cave entrance, by walking a little farther into the mouth of this cave, the entrance opened out in to maze of tunnels, some dead ends, some petering out to a few inches in depth, but the tunnels he had managed to walk down took him to deep within the mountain side, to hidden treasures he knew had never been discovered, and were his discovery and his alone.

Hands in his pockets, he kicked at the muddy pebbles in this porch-like space as the rain drummed its own symphony around him. As the stones scattered, he noticed something growing by the open arch. In the side of the cave/cliff, grew tendrils of green out of the rock from which hung ripe wild berries, dark red, and purple. He picked a few carefully, so as not to dislodge this remarkable plant hanging there, and popped them in his mouth. The bitter juice burst out to the walls of his cheeks and made him shudder. He swallowed quickly, pulling a face.

'Which way tonight?' he asked, the cave gently echoing its response. Walking the way his voice had suggested, the tunnel led him away from the rain in to the comforting yellow beyond. Scooping up a handful of glassy quartz in rose and crystal, greys and blues, he was transported back to sitting with a grey-haired teacher whispering a long forgotten fairy tale of breadcrumbs and gingerbread cottages, one of those stories that carried him through his miserable childhood, a story where good always prevailed and the evil parents were always brought to justice, the innocents were always rescued, and they all lived happily ever after.

Dropping his trail of stones one by one, he ventured deeper down the tunnel, the glinting stones leading his way or leaving his story-trail, he was not entirely sure which.

Shaking his head, water droplets rained down and he shivered clumsily before replacing his sodden baseball cap. Cold as he was, he was well prepared: waterproof jacket layered over jumpers, gloves at the ready in his pockets. He hadn't counted on this rain though and his face trickled wet making him shudder.

By his own reckoning, he had about two hours of daylight left and would need to be on his way back in one. Plenty of time to do what he had to do. Caves and darkness did not mix unless you were in the company of experienced cavers, those he watched many times blinking out from the entrances of Derbyshire caves, their eyes tiny in the daylight after hours of tunnelling their way through nature's stone mazes.

This cave was his favourite, for it hid deep within it his family's secret, his great granddad's secret passed down now to him and he held it tightly to his heart—the only family memento he could really cherish.

He smiled as he wandered the familiar path, the walls of the tunnel a soft yellow chalk, which when rubbed would be powder like icing sugar on to his clothes and the floor below.

Five minutes later and his cave changed completely. This was their secret and no one knew how to get beyond this space but him and his uncle now. Oh yes, and Holly, whom he had shown once before, his best friend in the world. The narrow tunnel gave way to a tiny room which when someone lay on his or her stomach and lowered themselves down, a diagonal chute could be within a larger chamber where the cave paintings hid away from the universe.

As a child, Ethan had wanted to draw his own story, adding to the comic strip spread before him; but thankfully, his uncle had stopped him and instead they had gazed at them, spoken about them, designed stories and lifetimes for these characters until they too were part of his family history. There was the child warrior, chasing a tiger or beast, his arm bent back wielding a dangerous spear, while another flew through the air to bring the beast down. A huddled group sat together, maybe cooking, maybe warming themselves by a fire in red and terracotta shades, black lines indicating movement of arms and legs as they prepared for supper. Many versions of these stories had evolved over the years, and Ethan treasured them all.

The heat from his body in this small space was starting to feel stifling. Ethan took off his jacket and tied it round his waist. He had forgotten to bring anything with him to drink and his throat started to crackle. He swallowed hard. This dwelling seemed dustier and darker than usual—maybe he had got his times wrong. If the sun set early, he'd be in trouble. Ethan rubbed his forehead where a warm throbbing had started. He needed water. In the corner of this space a tiny pool of rainwater had collected, clear despite being within this crumbling den. He scooped up a handful and drank noisily, his hand providing an unsuitable vessel. His knee knocked half a geode, almost cuplike in the way it was formed. He scooped up with this sparkling rock and drank, the liquid cooling his throat.

'That's better,' he smiled. He lay his hat down by the pool and stretched out his legs for a moment, his muscles tight after being scrunched up for so long.

The heat in the chamber was unusual and Ethan had never remembered being hot in here, his thin jumper now proving uncomfortable. He pulled his wet hat off again and threw it down.

Pulling at the neck of his jumper, he felt his body pulsate and a sickness claw his chest. Like when he'd fainted once through hunger and his teacher had put him in the staffroom until his mum had come to collect him. It felt like that again now. His mum had told him off for not fixing himself anything to eat, and the secretary had rather waspishly given her some 'free advice' whatever that was. Ethan had lain on that sofa all afternoon he remembered. But this was different. He felt sick but hot as well. The yellow walls were moving in and out and he wasn't sure he could breathe properly. He took a deep breath in and pushed it out through pursed lips like he'd seen them do on the telly.

Then, darkness.

# CHAPTER 16

# Holly

TRICKLES OF WATER ran down the cold pane of glass where Holly rested her head. The blue, purple, orange then red of the evening's sunset had now passed and the pale moon now took centre stage against its inky curtain. How long she had been there, she wasn't sure, yet day had turned to night as she'd sat there, wondering where Ethan could be. She had run all the way to the bus stop, yet he had gone, either home or to the caves. She just hoped he hadn't been so stupid. Her stomach hurt worrying about him as his absence from class was very unusual.

Ethan never took a day off school. He was never ill. He enjoyed the order school brought to his life so he never missed a day to skive off at home like some of her classmates occasionally boasted. For years, he had brought himself up, got himself to school on time, even at times of illness or broken limbs, the sanctuary was school and the order it brought to his life.

For Ethan to miss a day from school, his one constant, well, that was unsettling.

'No one's answering the phone, Holly,' the mousy secretary had blinked at lunchtime, when her curiosity and concern finally collided and a full morning without him had proved too worrying.

'No one will answer the phone,' Holly had scowled as she'd stomped back to afternoon registration. His mum would be sleeping off or topping up the gin. She was sure the school secretary had some knowledge of this, her cheeks pinking in hot spots as Holly had scowled at her in dismay.

Double English—an afternoon of Shakespeare. By then, Holly was convinced something was wrong. Pippa had understood Holly's angst, yet had tried to lighten the mood. 'Always a first time to get sick and stay in bed all day, Holly—don't stress,' she had smiled, in that serene way Pippa had. Petite and pretty with a short black bob, Pip was another ally in the class from hell that they belonged to.

'Today, class, we'll be looking at Lady Macbeth and her dreams. Will Shakespeare created this complex character then let us bear witness to her dreams. Who can tell me why Lady M's dreams may be an important device in this play?'

Dreams. Holly's stomach tightened as she recalled her own the night before.

*She had walked onward, in darkness, all night. Maybe the light ahead would take her out into moonlight, daylight. Maybe with every step, she just took herself farther away from any chance of escape. She had been lost in a maze of tunnels, no idea which way she was going: walls a dirty red-brown, biscuity in colour, and crumbly to the touch. Just like the babies under her feet disappearing one by one, as she tried to take hold of them, comfort them as they cried.*

'—one of her own. Holly, wake up!'

The class laughed.

'Daydreaming is not going to answer the question,' Miss Green smiled, a little exasperated.

'Sorry, Miss,' she blushed. 'I was just thinking about Lady Macbeth. I think her dreams were telling the audience that she—was dreaming about the murders?'

'We covered that, Holly.' The petite teacher shook her blonde waves and stood, hands on hips, waiting for a response.

Pippa kicked Holly gently and tapped the table. Her hastily scribbled note read: *It showed that the murders bothered her.*

'It showed the murders bothered her, Miss?' Holly asked, the perfect actress. She was sure to get the lead role at this rate.

'Finally, Holly. Your mum will be so pleased you managed to stay awake today.' Miss Green smiled and continued to address the class, writing student responses on the board. Nightmare . . . Guilt . . . Messages from her mind . . . Fear of being caught (reprisal) . . . Answers.

The answers lie inside. Her dreams were messages from her mind. Every answer to every problem she was ever to endure would lie in waiting, just ready to emerge when the time was right. They would present themselves as dreams.

But how was she to find those answers in her dreams when she wasn't even sure what the questions were? At school, her day was filled with finding answers by reading books, working out complicated equations and calculations. Some questions required a simple yes or no, while others were less black and white. Other answers could be different depending on your own history and experience or your upbringing.

The babies she dreamed of, were they good or bad? Were the babies to be cherished or removed? Were they a gift, or a hindrance to be wiped out forever? Her dream had been so real, yet she barely understood what it meant. Being so lost, too, wandering through tunnels with no sense of direction. What could that mean? She would have to go to Miss Sharp again after school and then she'd try to contact Ethan. She wasn't allowed to the house, but she might be able to walk that way after school. He had to be there. He had to.

'On Monday, we'll look through your findings and see what you bright buttons have all come up with. Okay? Any questions?'

Oh.

'It's okay,' Pippa whispered. 'I'll show you on the way home.'

'I can't, Pip, I'm sorry. I've got to go to the library.'

'Really?'

'And, Holly?' Miss Green called. 'Can you stay behind one minute, please?'

Oh. Rumbled again. Holly bit her bottom lip, eyes wide, making Pippa giggle gently.

'You are hopeless, Hol. Tell her you are looking forward to researching Lady M's dreams and you're covered.'

The class were gone in a few moments.

'I think we need a little chat, Holly. Come and sit here.'

Miss Green rarely missed anything. Few teachers cared if you took anything away from lessons, but Miss Green was different. She knew every child she taught and seemed genuinely interested in pushing her love of all things bookish on her students. Not only that, she seemed to care about the students she taught. They weren't just results and potential brainbox students. In fairness, the class' grades were rarely that. But Miss Green's classes were bearable.

'What's going on, Holly?'

'Nothing, Miss,' Holly lied, her cheeks hot under this spotlight of this teacher's interrogating eyes, kohl pencilled up to catlike perfection.

'Daydreaming is not unusual, Holly. You are not the first and you won't be the last. But I feel you weren't with us. Last year, you came in shining bright and I need to see that again. Anything that's bothering you? Life can change dramatically over the summer holidays. Anything I need to know about? Or can help you with?'

Her head tipped to the right, expecting a confessional.

'Nothing Miss.' Then, a 'light bulb' moment. Maybe. No. Ethan would kill her if he found out.

'No. Nothing, Miss.' She found a thread on her grey skirt's waistband and tugged at it gently.

'We're doing Macbeth, Holly. I defy anyone to sleep through my Lady Macbeth!' Smiling, she wrung her hands in the air. 'Will these hands ne'er be clean?!'

Holly relaxed and sat on the desk. Okay. Sorry Ethan. Deep breath.

'I'm just a bit worried about Ethan, Miss. He's not at school today and no one's answering the phone. Could you find out if he's okay?'

'I'm sure it's nothing, Holly. Let's see if he's back on Monday. Everyone's permitted a sick day occasionally.'

'But it's not like him, Miss. He doesn't like being at home . . .' Too much. Holly bit her lip and closed her eyes. Damn.

'Why, Holly?'

'Erm–'

'Tell you what,' this tiny teacher nodded, a plan formed in that instant. 'I'll ring now and see if there's a simple explanation. I've got a free period now and a pile of marking to avoid.' She winked, conspiratorially. 'If not, we'll get the Welfare Officer to pop in on the way home. Okay?'

That was not going to go down well. His mum hated visitors—especially anyone in authority. But, at least, she'd know Ethan was okay. 'Thank you, Miss.'

'Come to the office at the end of school. I'll meet you there.'

'Thank you, Miss.'

'My pleasure. Now off you go. Where do you need to be?'

'Double Maths.'

'Enjoy. And don't worry. Scoot!'

The corridors in school seemed longer than ever on a Monday, as the two final periods were at opposite ends of the school. She often thought roller-skates on the polished flooring would be a huge bonus, or a skateboard, just to speed things along. Some of the sixth formers carried their skateboards across the backs of their rucksacks, and Holly often imagined herself borrowing one and flying along to her next lessons.

'Holly!'

It was Miss Green.

'Sorry Miss—'

'Daydream believer?'

'What?'

'Never mind, you're far too young to remember that one. The Monkeys? Never mind. Miss Hutchins wants you to see you. Before your next lesson.'

'But I'll be late, Miss.'

'It's fine. I've spoken to Pippa—she's passing a message on. Mr B knows you're on your way.'

Holly sighed. 'What have I done?'

'Think of what you haven't done, Holly, and then you might be nearer the mark.' Miss Green tapped her arm reassuringly. 'You're not in trouble this time. Just go now. Quickly!'

Miss Hutchins' office was farther along the corridor, taking a left then a right past the school office.

'Oh, Holly! Miss Hutchins needs to see you!' came a shout through the serving hatch in the school office wall.

'Thank you, Miss. I'm going there now.'

Slightly unnerved by this new infamy, she knocked twice before turning the head teacher's door handle and walking in.

'Come in, Holly.'

'Thank you, Miss Hutchins.'

'Sit down, if you will.'

Holly sat hard down in the blue cushioned chair across from the rarely seen, rather formidable head teacher. Her desk sat between them like a mahogany wall, keeping each safe from the other.

'You are a friend of Ethan Davies? Year Six?'

'Yes, Miss.'

'It has been brought to my attention that Ethan did not go home last night. Do you know anything about this?'

Holly frowned in concentration. 'He didn't come back to school today, so I was worried. He might be ill.'

'He's not at home, Holly. This has now become a Missing Person Enquiry and may become a police investigation. This is very serious. If you know anything, I suggest you inform us immediately. Ethan could be in danger.'

Holly shrugged. 'I don't know, Miss.' Surely, he'd be back home now. He'd sloped off before when his mum was drinking, or his step-dad was being exceptionally vile, but only ever for a few hours and then he usually turned up again.

'We've spoken to your mum today and she's in agreement with us that you should head straight home tonight after picking up the boys from school. We may be dealing with an isolated incident here but all students will be advised to head straight home. Have you heard me, Holly?'

"Yes, Miss Hutchins.'

'No good ever comes from being a lone wolf, Holly. Let us help you. If you remember anything, I need to know. Okay?'

Holly nodded. So where are you, Ethan? 'Straight home, Miss. Got it.'

The head teacher briefly stood to usher Holly on her way before returning to her desk.

'And if anything springs to mind, Holly, anything at all, let us know.'

'Will do, Miss.' Holly left as gracefully as she could before running up the corridor to her next class.

The day dragged. Holly couldn't think of anything other than her friend, wondering where on earth he'd gone to.

'We can't just give up on him,' Holly whispered, as she and Pippa doodled their way through a particularly dull maths lesson.

'What can we do though?' Pippa asked. 'They've looked everywhere for him.'

'Well, not quite everywhere.'

Pippa's eyes widened as her friend sketched a map across a gridded page at the back of her maths book.

'*Where?*'

'Will you two get on with those algebra equations and stop gossiping? That sort of effort will not earn you good grades.' The teacher—a mass of beige in signature brown cords and matching jacket—frowned, his bushy eyebrows knitted together in disdain.

Drawing an x with a flourish, Holly pushed her drawing over to Pippa in response. 'There.'

'No way, Holly. You're mad. We're not going down there.'

Holly shook her head. 'It's the only other place he might have gone. What if stuff got so bad at home that he had to find somewhere fast? What if this was his only option? He might have fallen or got stuck—we need to check.'

'Tell the police,' Pippa mouthed.

'No,' Holly frowned. She knew those caves, the last bit of undiscovered Yorkshire, a secret hide-out. Should it be discovered, the whole area would be closed and barricaded as a place of national importance. Ethan would never forgive her. He had discovered those caves and entrusted her with the secret.

'What is it with you?' Pippa whispered, shaking her head. 'If you think he's there, you've got to let the police know. We can't go down there, it's dangerous. It should have been filled in or fenced years ago. I read something about it a few years ago—an anniversary report in the paper—about someone dying down there.'

'Rumour, rumour, rumour. Don't believe anything you see, hear or read, Pip. They never found her,' Holly corrected.

'Yeah, but police are trained. You are eleven years old. That's all I need to know on the matter. Just tell them what you think you know. You're up to something.'

'Just give me 'til tomorrow. I'll check out the place tonight and if there's nothing, then nothing's lost. Please, Pip. Don't breathe a word of this to anyone.'

'One day then,' Pip said, her lips tight. 'But stay safe, Holly. I mean it. If you're not in school tomorrow morning, I'm going straight to Miss Green. For sure.'

# CHAPTER 17
# Holly

A FIFTEEN MINUTE BUS RIDE later, she was at her destination: the caves Ethan had spoken of.

More a basin than a valley, the caves sat in the walls of this limestone feature, creating a circle of perfect hideouts for anyone who stumbled across it. But what Ethan had discovered in the summer months before, had secured a perfect secret for the two of them to bear. He had taken her there under oath that she would never breathe a word to a living soul. Very dramatic, was Ethan.

To the untrained eye, the space looked like the crash site of a meteor that had left a deep basin in the hillside. Certain caves, disappearing into the mountains by way of tunnel or maze, depending on how you approached it, became much more alluring the deeper the adventurer went further in, the more satisfying the prize. Etched on the walls were the most beautiful, untouched cave paintings of deer-like creatures being hunted by tall, brown figures with bows and arrows, woolly mammoth-type images, and fire paintings, hastily smoky chalk traces of reds and browns. How it had lain undiscovered for so long was more due to local superstition than anything else. Anyone who travelled deep in to the caves were always warned off, legend had it, by the beings that lived within the mountains protecting the treasures at the mountain's core. Coupled with a number of disappearances over the years, largely reported as caving accidents, the caves remained the subject of suspicion more than intrigue, and so few ventured there.

Holly had been only once with Ethan, that previous summer and neither were beaten by the threats of local folklore. They had found neither unhappy spirits nor deep mountain trolls beating their chests in a bid to drive them out by some magic power. It was the beauty of the cave drawings that had bought Holly's silence, and with that had somewhat sealed their close friendship forever.

Slipping gently on her descent, the soft sandstone shifted under her feet, making it impossible to stay upright. She slid rather ungracefully, her skirt tucked under her as she sped down to the bottom. Once in the depths of the basin, Holly ran past the first two entrances and slipped in to their favourite cave. Sitting down, Holly nodded to the cave's arched entrance as she did so, as was their tradition. She noted that someone had indeed been there, the remnants of a wooden fire and paper ash to the right of the first cave tunnel. She so hoped she was right.

Farther and farther in she travelled, the walls narrowing and the ceiling lowering to meet her, until the familiar images showed on the crumbling walls. Stooping lower, her elbows grazed the walls and chalky dust showered down on her. Her fingers stretched out in front of her, now feeling the way her eyes could no longer see.

Spluttering out what must have been a cobweb, she swept her hands left to right, then to left again, in a bid to clear the dark passage ahead. She could sense she was not alone. That sixth sense of hers could be getting her in to trouble again, she knew that, but it was impossible to resist. She followed where she knew there was company, hoping Ethan may be hiding out from his brothers or his volatile Dad.

'Hello?' she called, her voice carrying down the tunnel as the echo chased out of reach.

'Ethan, is that you?'

A scrabble of loose rocks suggested a positive response.

'Ethan?'

Following a faint scratching, perhaps a small animal, but hopefully her friend, Holly ventured deeper in, as the tunnel began to slope gently downwards. Holly coughed as the dusty air surrounding her caught her throat. One hand at her mouth and the other clutching her bag, Holly carried on in this half-stooped stagger until her back ached. Reaching down to the cold gritty floor, she sat down and opened her bag. Her fingers closed round the bottle of water and pulled it up to her mouth, gulping down the dust tickling her throat. She remembered as she touched the torch, and cheered as she realised.

Gentle yet vibrant sabre-toothed tigers chased by bow yielding hunters surrounded her as the yellow light clicked on. Even in this narrow channel, ancient travellers had taken time to etch these primitive cartoons, these moments in time.

One bow flew alone through the air—she wondered if the story's happy ending had been for the tiger or the hunter. Imagining the chase, the drama and the hopeful escape, Holly closed her eyes for a moment, her aching body heavy against the rock.

The light beyond her closed lids changed and she jolted. How long had she sat there?

The torch light was now more amber than white and it cast a strange dark glow around her. 'You stupid girl,' she muttered as she scrambled up and on her way. The tunnel seemed to be twisting left and still lowering steadily but she was sure she could still hear noise ahead of her. Tripping over a boulder, she stumbled, landing heavily on her hands. The burn of grazed knees took her breath away and she sat on the damp stone floor rubbing them through her thin, now torn tights.

'Ow.'

Blood seeped through, and the torch light revealed a purple splodge on each knee. Not a good look. Holly swung the torch round, its beam revealing only the way ahead and she pulled blue fabric from under a recently fallen pile of sandstone—a school baseball cap. Ethan had one. Underside there was no name, but she recognised the black marker ink E.T. written badly in the centre of the school badge. 'Oh, Ethan. When were you here? Where are you?'

Knees bloody and sticky, they caught against her woollen tights and made the crouched shuffle even more difficult. The hat's dusty coating of spiders' webs and cocooned flies told her that it had lain there for a matter of days and she was sure Ethan had had it with him on the first day of school. She remembered. Yes, he was wearing it last week. He's been here since then.

'Ethan? It's me, Holly. Just tell me if it's you—I'll feel stupid if you turn out to be a squirrel!'

Nothing.

In despair, she picked up a fallen chunk of sandstone and threw it down the tunnel into the hillside, illuminating its progress with the torch's fading beam as the rock bounced from wall to wall, deeper and deeper, quieter and quieter. Then nothing. This was pointless. No good at all. She should head back. An hour had passed and if mum were to suspect nothing, she would have to leave now. Her bus was due in 10 minutes and the journey up the basin side would be a damn side harder than her graceful slide down.

'Ethan, if you are there, show me now! I'll go, I'll happily leave you here if you're safe. It's me—Holly, your best friend. I won't tell anyone, I swear. I just want to know you are safe. I've got to get back really soon.'

She heard a distant scrabble, then another, and then . . . The same stone bounced back from its place beyond the tunnel and landed at Holly's feet. 'Aarrgh!' She jumped back, terrified. Someone, something was there, though what it was she had no clue.

'Ethan!'

A distant ripple of something—glass breaking, laughter—she wasn't sure. But that was not Ethan. All of a sudden, her courage left her and she turned. Tucking the cap in her bag, she scrambled her way back, her breathing fast and catching, as she held back frightened sobs. As her torch spluttered and she was plunged in to darkness, she stumbled her way through the tunnels until she saw the glint of twilight and her world once more, a world that was oblivious to the darkness unfolding.

## CHAPTER 18

# Holly

THERE WAS STILL no sign of Ethan. Miss Green, in her defence, had been true to her word and had rung up to see if Ethan's mum could shed some light on the whereabouts of her youngest son.

Apparently, 'How should I know?' was the sleepy, curt response. Social services had been informed as a matter of course.

A blur of History, Geography, Maths and Art had seen Holly tread along through the dark tunnel of her mind and her fear. Pippa occasionally jolted her out of her thoughts with a drink in the canteen or required her to copy down some notes.

The day's end couldn't come quickly enough as all Holly wanted to do was climb in to bed and sleep. Ethan's whereabouts were a complete mystery. Not at home, not at the cave, nowhere.

Glassy puddles led the way to Elmhill Primary and the journey flew as Holly strode along, lost in thought. It had rained hard the day before and the boys' Green Wellingtons Brigade had been a rather muddy affair, all the more muddy as the boys had forgotten to change into the wellington boots Holly had brought in for them the previous day.

'We got to dig for worms, Holly. Long, fat, juicy worms!'

'That's nice, Tom,' Holly answered, not really taking in her brother's jabberings.

'And we planted some herbs today–sage and mugwort!'

'Sage and mugwort!'

'What on earth is mugwort?!' Holly laughed, snapping out of her musings at last.

'Dunno, but sage is for cooking! Christmas stuffing in the Christmas turkey!'

'You learn some funny things at school, boys, that's for sure.'

*So where were you today, Ethan?*

'We planted more flowers. Blue ones.'

'Forget-me-nots and dusty millers.'

'Are you making these up?' Holly laughed.

'No, they are to make the garden safe and pretty at the same time.'

'What do you mean safe?'

'Dunno, maybe they don't hurt when you fall on them,' Jake shrugged.

'I've got something for you, Holly. I made it myself.'

Holly pushed the front door heavily and the boys spilled inside.

'Mum!!!'

'Hello my darlings . . . good day?'

'We planted forget-me-nots and dusty millers–'

'I made Holly a necklace.'

Mum lightly tapped the daisy chain around Holly's neck. 'It'll take more than daisies, Holly, to keep you safe. You'd better sit down. Boys, strip your muddy clothes off and put on the jeans I've popped at the end of your bed.'

'Is everything ok, Mum? Is it Ethan?'

The boys thundered upstairs.

'Are you telling me everything you know about Ethan?' Mum placed two hot mugs of tea on the table and took her place across from Holly. 'I had a call from school.'

'He could be in so much trouble, Mum. I can't say anything.'

'You can tell me.'

'He said it was all getting too much at home.'

'In what way?'

'Just with his step-dad and his mum. The usual stuff. I think he's had enough.'

'What happened when you went home last night? Was he okay then?'

Holly touched her lips as if to silence her mouth.

'What is it, Holly? This could be serious.'

'He goes to the Craglea Caves when things are too much. He wanted to go last night but it was raining. When I came out of school, he had gone and I thought he'd gone home. But I thought he might have gone there, and I went there but –'

'But what, Holly? Was he there?'

'Something was there. You're going to think I'm crazy, Mum, but there was something there. I called Ethan's name and –'

'You should not have gone there on your own, Holly. That was so dangerous. I'll ring the police.'

'He has a special cave, Mum, but no one can know about it –'

Cara tapped her fingers on the wooden table in annoyance. 'Holly, stop being silly. He could be lying at the bottom of the cliffs for all we know.'

'Don't ring the police yet, Mum. We could just go.'

'Let me sort the boys. Give me a minute.'

Cara rushed to the hallway and hid herself away while making a call. 'Thank you, Lucy. We'll be a couple of hours, max.'

A chill ran across Holly's back and into her bones, making her shudder. Wherever Ethan was, she needed to find him. The dreams of her falling down muddy slopes were all starting to make perfect sense.

## CHAPTER 19
# Holly

THE TWILIGHT BEYOND the crags had streaked its familiar pinks and greys as the two stood against the dramatic skyline.

Holly held Ethan's cap tightly in her hands, her face streaked in vertical pinks through the grime and the dust.

The silence hurt her ears and she clamoured for something to say, a way to explain how she knew Ethan was there and how he couldn't have got anywhere else, his body may be wedged in a small space yet unable to move back in to the tunnel in a bid to escape.

Police officers in smart blue uniforms slid down the embankment, swarming the area below like ants to a sugar bowl. They were everywhere, with lights and dogs–it was chaos down there and Holly felt so guilty that, despite Ethan's danger, the caves would soon belong to everyone. Although her mum denied involving the police, the place was swarming with them and they were refused entry to the caves on arrival.

'And your name is –'

'Holly. Holly Adams'

'My name is Sarah. I'm going to be looking after you this evening. We'll bring you and your mum down if the area is deemed to be secure.'

'But I can show you where to go? I need to show you.'

'We have our caving team–experts in their field, Holly. They are much better suited to the job. We will call you down should we need you.'

'But he's in there and it's getting dark–what are you waiting for?'

'All in good time, Holly. You say that you saw him?'

'He's deep inside, I can take you. Please let me show you.'

'We're just waiting for back up–they're on their way.'

PC Sarah strode up once more. 'Okay, Holly. We'll take you down and you can lead so far but you will have to stop when we tell you to. These caves are dangerous and the inner tunnels could collapse at any time. You are lucky to be alive.'

Stumbling down the familiar path, she fell ungracefully back over and over in her rush to get back down there, her hands gritty and bloody, covered in wet silt.

The canyon floor looked strange floodlit buzzing with police officers, and a caving team wearing helmets sporting headlights and thick orange overalls. Holly's chest constricted and her mind fogged suddenly and she leaned back in to her mum who was thankfully close by.

The lights and figures blurred through her wet eyes and Holly wished she was anywhere but here, back in her room with Ethan reading scripts or sitting in class through any lesson, it wouldn't matter. Anywhere but here doing this.

'Holly. Holly!'

She shook her head.

'Holly, we're ready.' The police officer shook her shoulder and an electric shock almost jolted her back in to the present. 'Lead the way Holly, until we stop you. Understand?'

'Yes.'

Her mum held her tightly. 'I'll be right here. Holly, I'm proud of you. Whatever happens, you have done everything you can.'

Feeling stronger somehow, she left her mum and started the walk to the cave.

'That's where I found his hat, the one I gave you.'

The cave entrance lit up as the camera whirred a collection of shots.

'We'll follow you, Holly,' PC Sarah assured her. 'Try to stay calm and as soon as you are ready, start speaking to Ethan. Tell him we are on our way.'

The tunnels narrowed and lowered, forcing the team down onto hands and knees. Holly took a deep breath and exhaled slowly.

'We're here, Ethan. I've brought help. We'll get you out of there.' Rolling her shoulders, she moved painfully through the tunnel. Her knees stung and her back seemed scratched and scraped from earlier, now hot with her jumper rubbing.

Nothing. No sound.

'It's not much farther.'

The sandy walls coated their shoulders, knees, backs and hands, with their yellow dust as the party moved steadily down the passageway. A ledge was partly visible and Holly knelt down.

'Ethan, can you hear me?'

Nothing.

'He's just down here. We need to shuffle down here to this drop then he's through there.'

She could hear the cavers talking with the police and quickly jumped down. 'Ethan, we're here!' Past the archway, she could see a blue fabric, the familiar edge of Ethan's hooded top.

'Ethan?'

The tunnels glowed with the artificial light flooding the tunnels, casting eerie shadows on the walls this way and that, multiplying the number of figures along the corridors.

'Holly?' He sounded so faint, whispering her name. But he was there.

'He's here! I heard him! Look there—just a little further then we'll be able to see him! There—do you see?'

Her body flat on the floor, she shuffled towards the opening beyond the ledge. Sharp fingers tapped her shoulder.

'We've got to get out, Holly,' another police officer stated. 'We need to let them get in to assess the area. The tunnels are damp and unsafe.'

'Did you hear him? He called my name.'

'Can you see him?' The police officer in charge, Sarah, crouched down to Holly's level and peered along the tunnel.

'Yes . . . well, not him but the blue of his sleeve because I couldn't get down to him. You stopped me. Let me show them.'

Three figures in orange were behind her and edging forward all the time. 'We'll take it from here, Ma'am.'

Holly wriggled free of this persistent woman's grip and shuffled forward once more. 'He's there–I need to show them! Let me go!'

Before she could say another word, Holly was on her feet being escorted firmly out of the way.

In one swift movement, the men in bright orange jumpsuits took her place, crouched in the small space, their helmet lights shining out, their faces obscured.

'He's in there, I heard him,' Holly shouted in to the white light. 'It's okay, Ethan, they're coming for you!'

Her arms were being tightly held as the group moved crab-like in formation back along the tunnels. Wriggling in a bid to get free, the two police officers tightened their hold around her, her arms pinned to her body, her feet barely touching the floor. Holly relaxed and let them guide her to the entrance. Her work was done. She had taken them to Ethan. And Ethan would be safe.

It was only when Holly was out in the artificial white light and the darkness beyond that she realised how late it must be getting. Warmth ebbed into her and she realised she was wrapped in brown woollen blankets. Shivering, her body wracked with deep tremors as she stood amidst the noise and the night. People everywhere, their dark blue uniforms lost in the darkness except for reflective strips here and there which jumped around like fireflies catching their prey.

An arm circled her shoulders and she flinched. Mum was there. 'You alright, love?'

Deep breaths. 'He was down there, Mum. I could hear him.'

'Okay, love.' Her squeeze tightened reassuringly. 'You've done everything you could.'

'I hope he's okay.'

Mum just held her as the events of the evening washed over her. They sat down against a nearby rock and cuddled against the bitter cold of the night, as the emergency services ran about like ants on a rock.

Holly closed her eyes. Exhausted, she leaned against her mum and saw, in her mind's eye, Ethan lying there cold and alone in that tiny alcove. At least she would see him again soon.

'Holly?' Shaken from her doze, she opened her eyes to Sarah. Her mum looked pale and tired, and the two women eyed each other, their expressions troubled.

'He's not there, love.' Her mum hugged her tightly.

'I saw his sleeve . . . his blue sleeve . . . he was definitely there.'

Sarah shook her head wearily. 'They've searched the area, the whole cave beyond the cavern we went to and there is no sign of him.'

Hot wet tears stung Holly's eyes. 'But he was there! I heard him!'

'Can we take Ethan's hat, Holly? We need to collect any evidence that shows he was there for our investigation.'

Her hand gripped the damp cap folded tightly in her pocket, slightly slimy now and mildewed after a night hidden away there. This was her talisman, her good luck charm, the only link with Ethan now.

Sarah held out her hand.

'Stop looking at each other like that. I saw him! I know I did.'

'It's late, Holly. Get home and spend the weekend getting some rest.'

Sarah gently pulled the blue baseball cap from Holly's hand and put it in a clear bag, like the type bought for sandwiches. She folded the top carefully and sealed Ethan's hat inside.

'Come on, love, let's go–they're going to take us home.'

'I don't understand, Mum. He was there.'

'Thank you, Mrs Adams. PC Daniels will take you both home.'

Holly shook her head. 'He was there. You didn't look carefully enough. Maybe you went the wrong way?'

'Our mountain rescue team are familiar with all the caves in the area. Your description was detailed and directions helpful, but your friend was not there.'

'Maybe he got out?' Mum suggested.

'There was no other trace of him apart from the hat you found. We need to match the particles on the hat with that in the cave. The boy has either escaped or–' she stopped and replaced her own helmet, 'perhaps you were mistaken.'

'No!' Holly shouted. 'I'm not making this up! He was there–I heard him and I saw him. That was definitely where he was.'

Holly felt her Mum's arm tighten round her shoulders, pulling her closer.

'That's as maybe, Holly,' Sarah sighed. 'Just get yourself home and we'll keep you updated if we have any news.'

'Thank you, sergeant.' Mrs Dawson pulled her daughter up and walked her steadily up the steep basin walls.

'I did see him, Mum,' Holly stammered. 'I don't understand. I really don't see how he could have got out.' It all felt so hopeless.

'These people are experienced cavers, Holly', Mum said through laboured breaths as they finally reached the top, 'much more adept than you're giving them credit for. He's not there.'

As they sat in the back of the police car, Holly's mind raced. Something was not adding up. Ethan could not have escaped, yet he had not been in the cave room when the cavers went in. Someone had moved him and she thought she might just know where he could be.

## CHAPTER 20

# Holly

WITH ETHAN'S SEAT in Maths and RE sessions left empty the next Monday morning, Holly's day dragged on through the teacher's monologue as she scribbled notes taking nothing in, her mind replaying the stone bouncing out of the cave on a loop. Terrified, yet determined, Holly knew she would be back at the caves before the day was out.

'I'll cover for you Holly, but if my mum finds out we're both grounded, man . . .'

Emma tucked her long black fringe behind her ear and shrugged her shoulders. 'I'll do whatever you want, Hol—you know that. Ethan's a mate. God knows what he's playing at, that's all I'm saying.'

'I really think he might go back there. He has nowhere else to go.'

'Wouldn't he go to yours though?'

'That's what I hoped but he's not turned up yet. I just need to check on him one last time.'

'Be safe, Holly. Weather's a bit rubbish though.'

Holly knew that she would need to go down to the old library to check in with Miss Sharp before she left the building. So much was starting to spin in her head, her dreams, the faeries, Miss Sharp and Mr Bartholomew.

'I need to do my homework, Emma,' she lied on the way out of school. 'I might just go to the library now.'

'I'll come with you,' Emma nodded. 'You need a friend.'

Holly was glad of the company, and smiled. It had been so hard, missing Ethan and worrying so much about him. Emma was a good friend, as Holly knew she wasn't the greatest friend to be around right now. Her chest hurt whenever she even thought about Ethan. The loss and pain was like a sharp stab to her chest. She'd never felt anything like it. She seemed to go through the day in a fog, half thinking about things and never getting anywhere.

Emma linked arms with her and they walked to the old oak room together.

'Holly. I hoped you'd come.' The small figure of Miss Sharp stepped out from the gloom of the book shelves and took her hand. 'How are you my dear?'

'Hi Miss Sharp. We're just here to do homework. Do you know Emma?'

'Yes, my dear,' she peered over her half-moon spectacles up at her and smiled. 'Music is your passion–and witchcraft–you're often sitting in those sections!'

'I suppose so,' Emma smiled, wrapping her black cardigan tightly around herself.

'Why don't you set up and I'll join you in a second? I just want to talk to Miss Sharp about something.'

'I'm in no rush –'

'Go on my dear,' Miss Sharp encouraged, her hands wafting Emma towards the comfy leather chairs away from them.

Emma smiled and walked away, no questions, no gestures.

'I'm so worried about Ethan' Holly started, as soon as she could be sure they were alone. 'I know he was in the caves–did they tell you I showed the police? But they now think I'm crazy as they couldn't see him.'

'Faerie magic mists the eyes, Holly,' Miss Sharp nodded. 'Surely, you worked that one out for yourself? Remember what we read last week?'

'That's nothing like this . . . what are you suggesting? Miss Sharp– this is madness.'

'I'm preparing you, my dear. There is nothing you can do but wait. I'm so sorry.'

Holly caught the bus out of town, texting her mum that she would be at a revision session in the library for the next four hours with Emma, who was now working alone there. Emma would be there anyway, hidden in the Magic and Folklore section on her favourite leather sofa, its deep burgundy in keeping with the curiosities on the surrounding bookshelves. A perfect alibi if ever she was to need one.

The rain was falling once more, steady light rain this afternoon, and Holly closed her eyes tightly hoping for it to stop. She couldn't possibly imagine what was going through Ethan's mind when he left for the caves. Why had he decided to come down here in this rain? Now on its third day of refreshing and battering them in equal parts, persistently muddying all the pathways, making waterfalls of the stony slopes and tiny reservoirs in the uneven pitted basin of the pit.

As the rain ceased, her bus pulled in to the lay-by for her and she jumped down awkwardly, narrowly missing a large puddle. Dripping and sparkling fresh from the downpour, Holly inhaled the heady tree-pollen perfume and began her descent.

*Where are you, Ethan?* After finding his cap the previous day, Holly knew he had been here, as recently as Tuesday, yet there seemed to be no trace of him. It was possible he had ventured into another cave, but this was very unlikely. A thorough search of the caves had been fruitless and Holly had resigned herself to the fact that he had not been there on Friday. He was nervous of the caves, aware of the fate open to anyone exploring without a guide who knew the ways the tunnels led away from safety and fresh air, towards unsafe floors and underwater pools where once trapped inside, a traveller's fate would be sealed.

He had to be sleeping there–he had nowhere else to go if he wasn't at home and he'd not turned up on Holly's doorstep. She would search the cave until dusk. It was all she could do.

Slipping on the wet sandstone, she steadily lowered herself to the floor and eased herself down the sliding mountainside towards the basin. Not a sound. The rain had battered the area and it shone glossy and new, yet the usual bird song was missing. The heavy sky threatened its next downpour and Holly knew she didn't have long. Ashen clouds rolled along directing her towards the caves, swelling and rolling as they accompanied her on her way. Within minutes, Holly was running towards the mouth of the third cave.

Her heavy black boots missed their footing and Holly fell forwards, hands outspread to meet the sharp, gritty sandstone. She remained there on all fours waiting for pain. Her hands smarted and her already scabbed-over knees screamed their own protest, but Holly's attention was elsewhere. Carefully placed stones–white, rose, milky amber– some quartz she thought, led her into the mouth of the cave. Rose, milky white, amber; rose again, the colours varied but this seemed to indicate some sort of trail. Maybe just coincidence, but her mum had always said there was no such thing as coincidence. Could this be Ethan's handiwork in some Hansel and Gretel bid to help him find his way home?

'I'm here, Ethan!' She yelled stumbling up to her feet. 'I'm coming!'

Her school uniform afforded no real protection from the narrow tunnels, but Holly could not think about that now. Before long, she was deep within the tunnels once more, following this trail of stones, leading her to her friend she desperately hoped. With her grey school skirt gritty with the wet, yellow sandstone, her woollen tights thick with blood at the knees once more, she pushed on. Finding Ethan would excuse her, she was sure, and a little washing powder would clear her name. Deeper still and the dull yellow of the torch gave little comfort. It wavered slightly in the darkness. Shaking it gently, it ebbed its light a little brighter. It mustn't desert her now.

'Ethan!' The tunnel lowered at an almost diagonal slope but then stopped. Ahead was the tiniest shelf but there was no way she could fit through there or even attempt it. She was not familiar with caving and had only once before pushed herself through such a gap years before, on a school adventure holiday with two tutors helping her through. Ethan, however, would have had other ideas. With her blazered elbows dusty and hair full of cobwebs, she lowered herself on her stomach down to the gap and shone the last dull beams through the gap.

'Ethan? Are you there?'

The beams scanned the chamber beyond this letterbox of a gap. He could have squeezed through at a push, though why he would have wanted to was beyond Holly. The light fell on what looked like a grey shape, maybe a leg, but most definitely fabric. Her torch beam shone left and up a little.

Hot angry cheeks, wet wide eyes and a stern line of a mouth revealed themselves.

'Ethan? Is that you?' Thank goodness he was alive.

'Get me out of here. Please. Help me.'

'We were here yesterday, but the police were hopeless. They sent the search party home. They said I was deluded and traumatised or something. Why couldn't they see you when I led them right to you?'

'They were here. I called out but they left. I'm done for, Holly. I can't feel my legs.'

'Are you hurt?'

'Help me, Holly. I can't feel anything. But I can't move.'

'Miss Sharp, the librarian, she reckons this is some kind of weird faerie magic. It's all stupid and crazy. I don't know what to believe.'

She pushed her arm as far as it could reach in to the chasm, her head and shoulder splayed against the wet rock. 'Can you give me your hand? I could try to pull you out.'

'*I can't move!*' He almost spat the words at her and she felt his temper rise in him like a tornado, hot and wild as panic took over. 'Get me out of here! I can't move!'

She squeezed again, her cheek grazed against the stone, her knuckles bleeding against the sandpaper walls. 'I don't know how to–you're going to have to move a bit closer, Ethan. Just try.'

He blinked as the torchlight faded to a low amber glow, his body rigid as stone. 'Just get to me, Holly. Can you reach me at all?'

Hot tears sprang down her cheeks. It was hopeless. 'I can't. I'm sorry.'

'Don't say that, Holly. You have to.'

With the torch propped up against the ridge, she pushed again, this time forcing her shoulders low and her rib cage in to the ground. Her head was almost through and her arm reached out towards

Ethan's limp hand. He was cold to the touch and did not respond to her as her fingers curled around his outspread hand.

'I'm here, Ethan, I'm here.'

Quiet sobs, slow, controlled, exhausted sobs wrenched from his unmoving body and Holly held his hand quietly until he stopped.

'How can I get you out of there?' she whispered. 'I just can't see how I can get you out.'

He couldn't even hold her hand, Holly realised, never mind clamber out of this place, this hole where he'd been lying for goodness knows how long. He lay against a stone curve in the cave wall, curled against it with his legs outspread. His head rested unmoving while his eyes darted wildly towards her, staring out from a much thinner pinched expression, willing her to save him. Streaky with tears, his face betrayed his terror and she jolted in to action.

'It's okay, Ethan. I can get you out, but I need some help.'

'Don't leave me here, Holly. Don't leave me. Please.'

'If I stay, we'll both die of the cold. It really is the only way. Be brave, Ethan. I'll be an hour at most.' She squeezed his hand reassuringly and moved away. A defeated grunt followed her out of there. The cold was taking him and she knew she didn't have much time.

'Something is stuck in me Holly – it really hurts. Can you see what it is?'

She had barely registered what lay on his stomach, curled up and still, but as she shone the torch beam closer, she noticed something. Nesting. Curled up between his rib cage and his navel lay a sleeping creature covered lightly in downy fur. Its body rose and fell in a silent rhythm.

Just as Miss Sharp had read to her the day before. 'Ethan, how does it feel?'

'It really hurts. It's in me, like stuck in me—I can't move but it feels numb and hurts like hell all at once. You've got to get me out, Holly. Please don't leave me.'

Her torch flickered and its orange beam dulled as its power lessened. In the ebbing light, it was difficult to see what had made its home with him, yet with each dull yellow light that pulsed, she made out arms and legs and a delicate face not unlike that of a tiny human baby, hauntingly beautiful.

'One hour, Ethan. I promise.'

'You won't be back. If you leave me, I'll die here.'

She edged backwards along the tunnel once more, the wet stone slowing her journey, her back grazing the walls and ceiling as she twisted and turned through her ascent to the surface, the pain catching in her throat.

'Holly? Are you there?'

'I'm okay, Ethan. Not long now . . .'

'Don't leave me, Holly. Please!'

But his voice was distant, exhausted and faint. The oxygen would run out soon if the cold didn't get him first.

## CHAPTER 21

# Holly

HOLLY RAN FROM the cave, her mouth dry, her head spinning. Standing in the basin, surrounded by caves and cliffs, she felt momentarily as an ant must feel after scurrying out from underground into bright daylight and possible danger. The light had started to fail and Holly knew she had to act quickly. Her head spinning, she slowed her breathing in and out while she planned her next move. What should she do?

Suddenly, a force pushed her downwards, her legs went from under her and she fell crumpled in to the dust. She gasped, surveying the area. Holly was completely alone.

She must get to the bus stop. Back there, she could alert the driver. He would almost certainly have a phone and call for mountain rescue, an ambulance, whoever they called in instances such as these.

The basin stretched up away from her and her spinning thoughts slightly hindered her focus. Fingers reached up to grasp rock, ledge, grassy verge to lever herself up on her way. The earlier rain made the job much more difficult, but the gradient was gentle at first and she carefully made her way.

Her boots found foot holes easily and Holly pushed herself up carefully, making allowances for the mud and the slime. As long as she took it steady, she should be okay. The first few metres went without error. Hands pulling on clumps of wet grass and mossy plants proved tricky and she slowly edged her way up, her hands fumbling and her feet slipping awkwardly at each stage. Pulling wayward flowers and stalks out of the crevices sometimes gave her somewhere to place her gritty fingers and give her a little more control. Pulling herself up to the next hand holes, she realised the basin had begun to lean away over her and no longer afforded her the gentle slope up to the top. She was way out of her depth now with nowhere to go.

To her left, the cliff seemed to reach up and back, sloping again as she had earlier predicted. She needed to get to that section. Easing to the left, she cautiously shuffled along a tiny ridge in the rock where pale yellow flowers peeped out. Her hands grazed the sharp ledges as she reached up again, ignoring the needles of pain across her fingers and ripping in to her nails. She had to make it across to this ridge.

Pushing her fingers in to a narrow crevice, her cuticles and skin ripped back against the sandpaper stone. The pain made her gasp and pulling her bloody hand back, her balance was thrown. Holly felt her body peel away from the rock face and then there was nothing.

How long she had lain there was anybody's guess. She woke as if from a deep, groggy sleep, aware of a pain in her right hand and a throbbing along the side of her head. As sensation returned to her, she seemed to be lying on something soft and she pushed down. She lay on what felt like short, soft grass, cushioning her and tickling her right cheek and arms.

She had fallen backwards, out from the cliff face down in to the chalky pit below, yet her body lay face down on grass. Opening her eyes, she realised darkness had fallen and the silence surrounding her was only broken by her breathing.

Could she move?

She wriggled her left fingers, then her wrist, before bending her outstretched arm at the elbow. With much effort, she painfully moved her right hand, still smarting from the graze she had sustained earlier.

Pushing herself up on all fours, nothing hurt to suggest she had broken anything, which in itself was remarkable. How far had she fallen?

No cliff or mountains above her. No basin of caves surrounding her. No chalky floor beneath her.

She was sat in a grassy clearing within what seemed to be woodland. Elm trees towered above her at intervals, all around her lit by a soft milky moon overhead.

But how?

Holly remembered falling back away from the cliff face yet nothing from that point. As hard as she could, her mind offered nothing.

Her hands were clean and scratch free, no evidence of the earlier trauma she'd endured climbing her way out of the basin. Holly hugged her knees tightly and shuddered. This place seemed strangely familiar but she wasn't sure how.

In the grass, a short distance away, a red-and-white toadstool peeped out–one of those fly agaric toadstools she'd learned about on a nature walk years ago at primary school. Holly smiled. This familiar sight comforted her and she leaned towards it only to find its neighbour centimetres away. And another. And another. A row of tiny toadstools, their white spots reflecting in the moon glow. Her mum had once told her how the parent toadstool would release spores away from its centre casting a circle of infants all around it before dying away in its centre. Sometimes, a full circle of toadstools would grow, holding magical properties and were where the fairies of her bedtime stories would congregate to dance. The curve of toadstools wound round her as she turned, revealing a perfect circle. It was within this circle that she'd come to find herself. Shaking herself in to full consciousness, she reached out and traced the circle around her.

'Hello?' she whispered, blushing at the very idea that someone could be out there. But then this situation really couldn't get any more curious. Someone or something had brought her here. That, she was sure of.

The ache in her head now returned with some force and she pushed at her right temple to ease the pain. An image of Ethan flashed before her, her memory of him trapped in the rock merging with a softer, slowly ebbing image all pastels and soft focus. His green eyes looked out at her directly as if he could see her, his body distorted by moving, turning shapes like a kaleidoscope before him. The image faded, replaced by the elm ahead of her, the pastel shapes replaced with flowers at the base of the tree, living flowers in every pastel shade tied tightly with long fern fronds.

As she looked around her, nine other elms stood guard, each one bearing a garland of flowers, each one brittle and in various stages of decay, their decorations placed there at different times, years before. Flowers were placed like this for the dead, Holly remembered, and these were testament to someone, somewhere, a shrine perhaps.

Ten trees, ten shrines—one with fresh flowers to mark a new death. The thought caught hard in her throat. Ethan.

She had to get back to him but how? She didn't know where she was or what this meant, but she was sure Ethan was in terrible danger and she no longer knew what anybody could do to help.

Her head felt heavy, full of this responsibility. Nothing made sense anymore. Her waking hours and dreams were muddled. Baby faces in her head again, the memory of Ethan in the cave, the creature sleeping in his chest—what did it all mean? Speaking to Ethan, knowing he was trapped—a prisoner of something otherworldly.

Placing her hands in the wet grass, she started to get up. A light darted from behind the tree with fresh flowers and moved swiftly to the next tree. Then the next, then the next. As it darted from tree to tree, Holly moved round, her knees wet in the cushioned grass, not daring to take her eyes from the light, not daring to blink, not daring to look away.

*One decade past, a child is lost*
*For faerie lore decrees*
*A changeling lives a decade long*
*Once the human child is seized.*

*They live a whispered half life*
*Once human babes are gone*
*Two lives we take, your freedom to make*
*The moon child will live on.'*

Holly had heard that song before. Narrowing her eyes, she repeated what she could remember.

*They live a whispered half life*
*Once human babes are gone*

104

*Two lives we take, your freedom to make*
*The moon child will live on.'*

'The moon child will live on,' whispered a voice and Holly spun round to face it—the same glass-like tinkling laughter echoed around the trees. The elm leaves moved suddenly, a hard breeze, as if a tiny whirling had spun up from there and disappeared off beyond the circle of trees.

'Hello?' Holly called, 'show yourself to me. Please tell me what this has to do with Ethan. I really don't understand.'

Nothing. Holly could have slept and been visited by one of her nightmares—she knew. Yet her heart tugged heavily and Holly knew Ethan and Bette must be linked. And somehow, she was linked too.

Beyond the trees, a wall—bottle green ivy clambering over russet red brick—the colour tugged at her sub-conscious. Lightly stepping out of the toadstool ring, Holly carefully walked past the trees, watching for observers, captors, she was now sure she was not alone. The high wall shielded this secret place—a hidden garden full of secrets and magic. Holly needed to get out and find her way back to the caves, but she knew she could be anywhere. Walking along the wall's perimeter, Holly came to a black wrought-iron gate, its rusting metal twisted and curled in pretty leaves and flowers. Pushing hard, the gate moved slowly and creakily, allowing only an inch or so access. Thorns and thistles scratched at her ankles as she stepped over them, this gate seemingly left unopened for some time. She heaved and pressed the heavy metal structure until it gave enough space for her to squeeze through, and she fell exhausted on the other side. Wet grass. Dripping trees. Daisies along the wall and around her now as she lay in the damp grass. The lawn spread away from her up a hill, and to her right, lay the Healing Garden she had visited earlier that week. Holly picked herself up and ran. A panic was quickly forming in her chest and she knew time was not on her side. Up the hill she ran, her bruised and scratched legs flailing through sheer exhaustion, the earlier climbing and her fall. The hill raised up at quite a gradient, and her calf muscles protested as she made it to the top.

Elm Hill Primary School, its Victorian towers and orange red brick stood silent, closed and dark, lit gently by the full moon overhead. The perimeter fencing securing the school with its dark green spikes and narrow steel lines would deny her access through its grounds, yet the sheer relief that she knew where she was, was enough for Holly. The rows of terraced houses surrounding the school were well known to her and the layout would allow her a way home. A short distance from the field, Holly scrambled up over a high wall, and lying across its top looked out over the estate where this school was at its centre. In silence, with the stealth of an alley cat, Holly ran between gardens and driveways over hedges and low-lying walls, until she came to her road.

With her house key poised, she ran up the steps to let herself in. The door opened.

'Where the hell have you been?' It was her mum. 'I've got the police out looking for you!'

'Mum, I'm sorry–I need to tell them . . .' Her pleas were cut off as she was pulled tightly in a bear hug while her mum relayed the panic, the danger, the search party, and so on.

'Mum–it's Ethan. I have to tell them where to go. They can't have been looking properly. He was just where I said he'd be.'

Her mum switched the hall light on. 'Look at the state of you. Now tell me where you've been. And this better be good.'

Sitting at the kitchen table, wrapped in her favourite blanket, Holly explained as best she could what she had seen, sipping hot chocolate at intervals and omitting the last part about waking up behind her brothers' school. She gave as much detail as she could and sobbed as her mum relayed the details once more to police and mountain rescue over the phone.

'Just try to get some sleep, Holly,' Mum whispered when all the necessary calls had been made. Holly could hear the one last call ringing on and on when ringing Ethan's house. 'I'll try Ethan's mum again in the morning.'

When sleep eventually came, her troubled dreams were filled with quartz stone trails, toadstools and decayed flower garlands and the image of Ethan trapped below ground waiting for her to return.

## CHAPTER 22

# Ethan

T HE DUST ON his breath caught sharply in his throat and he awoke coughing. He saw again the room that was now his prison, the space he had clamoured to now would be the last place he saw. He seemed to be in the same position he'd fallen asleep in that first night. He'd lost movement in his arms and legs since. The low ceilinged cell of sandstone seemed smaller in this dim light.

An ache spread across his lower back again, as had been the pattern over the last few days, creeping around his right hip and tightening in to his side. He knew he must have fallen at a very strange angle as his body protested at regular intervals, maybe every five minutes or so, although time now meant nothing. No sunrise, no sunset, no trailing sun in the sky to alert him to his place in the timeline of his day.

His arm still remained trapped under his left leg although he tried with every ounce of his energy to move even slightly. It was no use.

Why hadn't they come through yesterday? He had heard Holly shouting, screaming, being dragged away and then nothing. A series of faces at the opening had peered in and looked straight through him, ignored his calls, his cries, his desperate pleas, before they had all turned away taking the light with them back out in to the open far away from him in this cold dank space.

All hope was draining away now, he knew, as the cold took over and the creature embedded within him was growing stronger. Who or what it was terrified him, and exhausted him beyond care in equal measure. The freezing cold had numbed all pain and was beginning to numb all fear and loss in him now as he lay here in this unlikely tomb. Occasional chinks and splashes broke the silence, which was now all he lived for, counting between them in a bid to make some sense of how long he lay here.

The sharp pull in his chest again—he no longer protested—then the dull ache subsided to nothing. He had wondered at first if the creature was just flexing a contented claw, like Holly's cat often did deep in to his lap, but he'd learned that this was no cat. This sleeping creature was otherworldly, perhaps a deep cave dweller like a bat or a mouse, yet much longer and stranger than anything he'd seen before. The pain suggested it had hooked itself in to him somehow and he feared that this would be the death of him. It was most certainly the cause of his paralysis.

Surely he wouldn't just be left here to die, immobile and alone, save for this strange companion, living on him and accompanying him in his final hours. Surely soon, someone would rush in and wrap him up in warm woollen blankets, take him home to where his mother would have sobered up for fear of losing her youngest child as she had her eldest a decade before, she would take him in her arms and promise everything would be better, happier, much more like Holly's family, the family who had chosen Holly and made her their world.

The creature snuggled in sharply, connecting deep inside him and Ethan winced, no energy left to protest. Yet who would hear his cries now? He was merely supporting this new life and his time was almost up. He would most likely perish here to be cast aside like a shell when this strange being was ready to flee the nest it had created within him. So much he didn't understand. So much more he had hoped for himself than this. His heart ached and he slept once more.

## CHAPTER 23

# Holly

BEFORE THE SUN rose the following morning, Holly had woken and fallen again in to dreams many times. *Ethan lying there, his nails clawing at the cold crumbling rock, as he lay alone terrified. Ethan's hat, dusty and cold, held tight in her hands as she ran down endless corridors.* She woke to the dark of her bedroom, closed her eyes briefly to find herself scouring corridors once more. She barely knew reality from dreams in these night-time terrors. Finally waking to the early morning sun, her head spun and her eyes scratched tight and sore.

'The boys are staying with Felix's mum, Lucy, again today. I need you to rest today, my darling. If you feel the way you look, you need a day at home. I'll ring school and I'm sure they'll understand.'

The local news played out on the small silver radio on the sideboard as Holly curled up on the old battered sofa and rested her head on her favourite mossy green cushion. Its scratchy knit was bearable and she welcomed the discomfort. If only Ethan was safe. By bearing the itch she could perhaps trade for Ethan's homecoming.

As a small child, she would lower herself in to a hot bath, enduring pain and possible scalding to trade off with God that her mother would be healthier, Ethan's sister would come skipping home... None of it had ever worked.

'Can I get you anything, Holly?'

'I'm fine, Mum.'

'You're not fine my darling, but you will be. We've come too far already.'

'When you found me, Mum, when you found me all those years ago, tell me the story.'

'You've heard it a thousand times, Holly. I think you need to rest.'

'I can rest while you tell me. Come and sit with me, Mum. I need a cuddle.'

'Budge up then.' Mum nestled down in the sofa cushions and they curled up together. She gently stroked her precious daughter's hair and sighed.

'I had wished for a child, Holly. So many times. You were a gift.'

'I often wonder who my mum was. If she was much older than I am now, if she was frightened, why she left me there.'

'You were a wanted child. I wanted you so much. It was just fate that I found you.'

'Or moon magic, Mum! You said you wished for me.'

'Don't say those things, Holly. People will think we're mad.'

'But don't you sometimes wonder where I came from?'

'I know where you came from. Fate brought us together. If we remember that, the rest fades away.'

'What do you mean?'

'Nothing, Holly.' Her mum went to stand up.

'Tell me the story, Mum. Please. No more questions.'

'I had wanted a child so much, so much it hurt. I often went up to the castle, all times of the day and night. I liked to be on my own and your dad was always away; Sally was preoccupied with her baby, so I needed somewhere to go.'

'Bette. Was Bette still there?'

'Yes. Bette disappeared later. It was a very difficult time.'

'Don't you ever think it was a bit weird though, Mum? That you found me and Bette disappeared? Did anyone ever ask you about that?'

'No more questions, you said. And no. Coincidences happen all the time. You're being silly.'

'Right. But I thought you said there are no such thing as –'

'Do you want me to carry on?'

'Ok. Sorry.'

'This particular night . . .'

'. . . the night of the full moon . . .'

'This isn't a fairy tale, Holly, but yes, I remember it was a full moon as the castle was lit brightly with moonbeams, that's how I found you.'

'That's quite magical.'

'What are you going on about, Holly? Stop with all this nonsense.'

'I'm just saying Mum, it's a saying – like it was special.'

Cara sighed deeply. Her chest hurt with all this questioning. 'I found you. Under the light of the moon, beneath a holly bush in the old overgrown moat of the castle. You didn't cry, you just looked up at me and I thought you were beautiful.'

'What did Dad say? When you brought me home? You've never told me.'

Cara stroked her daughter's hair. They had argued. She would never tell her daughter that she was the reason they fell out and never quite managed to make the marriage work after she brought her child in to the house. She would never tell a living soul how he couldn't bear to pick up this longed for child who had been given to her. Cara knew Holly was no stranger's baby. She was her baby. Given to her in return for her co-operation. Her silence. The village had so many secrets and their lives were part of the village's secrets now. No one must ever know. She could never really be sure, but recent events were causing all those old worries and anxieties to rise up in her again. Only this time, her crazy thoughts were making a lot more sense.

'Let me make you some hot lemon and honey.'

'I haven't got a cold. I miss Ethan. I feel frightened for him. I don't think a hot drink is going to fix this.'

'I know, my darling. But we have to keep going for everyone else. You have to keep strong for Ethan.'

'Do you think he's ok, Mum?'

'I don't know, sweetheart. But I know that we will keep looking for him, won't we? Just when you're feeling a little stronger. The police are out looking for him and I know his mum will be doing everything she can . . .'

'. . . Drinking everything she can, you mean. She's just going to get worse.'

'That's unkind, Holly. She has had such a lot of sadness in her life.'

'But don't you think it's weird that Bette disappeared and I was found? What if she was taken by the same person who dumped me?'

'*That's enough!*'

'Mum, just listen—what if Bette was taken and I was just left there?'

'Don't you ever say such things again, Holly. Now get yourself dressed and back to school if you're well enough to be making such wild accusations.'

Holly stood up, her face hot and her fists clenched. 'You are being a bit extreme, Mum. I'm just saying what people must have thought at the time. I'm not being difficult. It's not an accusation – I know you aren't anything to do with this. You just found me.'

'That's right. This is not my fault.'

'But, what if Ethan has been taken by the same people who took Bette? Ten years have passed—why aren't the police doing more about that?'

'Holly. Enough. Don't you ever talk about this again. You're trying to make sense of nonsense. Leave it to the police. Now, are you going back to school, or are you going to shut up and rest?'

Holly sat down on the settee. It was no use trying to talk to her mum when she was in this frame of mind. 'I'm sorry if I upset you, Mum. But I was just talking. That's all.'

Cara wiped the hot tears from her cheek and shook her head. 'Are you happy now?'

Cara's head spun and she walked quickly away, leaving her daughter in the next room. Exhaling through tight lips, she leaned against the quietly closed door and let the tears fall. It was closing in. It was all closing in. Her house of cards was falling down and if she wasn't careful, it would be her daughter, her most precious prize, which would cause its collapse.

How she would slow, or stop the chaos find her again was something she needed to work out. And fast.

## CHAPTER 24

# Holly

*E*THAN'S DISAPPEARANCE, THE subsequent cave search and failed rescue had made the headlines, yet Holly felt empty. Ethan's rescue had been foiled purely due to the rescue team not looking carefully enough, of that Holly was sure. How could they not have seen him a second time? She had spent the rest of the day listening to the radio for any more news. She couldn't concentrate on a book or even the reading of her Oliver Twist script. That just made her think of poor Ethan.

There had been no report on the fact that this was the second disappearance from the same family, although she was sure it wouldn't be too long before Ethan's Mum would be called in again to speak to the police. She had been avoiding them, something she'd heard her Mum talking about the other day, yet who could blame her? All Holly wanted to do was curl up in a ball and pretend this wasn't happening. Ethan's mum had to deal with this in the knowledge that this had all happened once before, ten years ago.

Holly needed to go back to the caves and back to the Healing Garden. She was sure something was happening beyond the normal sleepy goings on of the village. As much as mum had explained away her being placed in the healing garden, it made no sense. She knew something linked the two places and she somehow had triggered something. Or maybe she had been sent away from the caves as she was a little too close for comfort. Holly knew that there was only one way to solve this and she would have to go back there herself.

As the boys got ready for school that morning, Holly dressed in her school uniform quickly and pushed a few things in her school rucksack. Diary, torch, and her secret stash of raisins from her bedside table drawer, just in case she needed a snack. As the three of them tumbled downstairs, Holly prepared herself for battle.

'What are you doing dressed for school? I think you need another day at home.'

Holly sat down at the kitchen table and poured the square shapes in to her cereal bowl. 'I'm fine, Mum. I'm better back at school. I'll drop the boys off on my way.'

'Careful with the milk, Holly,' Mum called. White liquid spilled past her bowl and onto the table. "You're not ready to go back – you're all over the place.'

'I slipped, Mum. Stop fussing.' The paper towel soaked up the mess and Holly proceeded to eat, shovelling the cereal in to her mouth as quickly as she could.

'Have a quick cuppa then, Holly. Just slow down a bit. The boys have got ages yet.'

As she placed her bowl in the sink, she nodded. 'Ten minutes, Mum. But no more. I just need to get in to school – I thought I'd prepare my English essay on Macbeth. It's easier if I'm in the school library if I need to check anything.'

'Drink this.'

The hot amber liquid swirled opaque in the earthenware mug, Mum's favourite, and it tasted good. Slowing down was never easy for Holly. She had so much to sort out and needed to get to the Healing Garden, the caves – too much to check out and far too little time to do this.

'Do you remember when I woke up in the Healing Garden? I came home and you wouldn't let me tell the police. Why was that? Surely, if someone had put me there, the police need to know. That could be a link to whoever has Ethan, Bette . . .'

'You're doing it again, Holly. You're meddling. Please stop. You have no idea what you're doing and the police are the experts.'

'So let's tell them! Let's explain what happened and they can come with me to retrace my steps – there might be evidence at the caves, at the school garden – we might be helping someone hide Ethan by not saying anything.'

'Drink your tea and go to school. Leave the amateur dramatics to that English teacher of yours. I can't keep going round in circles. You must let this go, Holly. Bette and Ethan, they're gone. Hopefully, they're safe, but we will go mad if we keep on like this.'

Not for the first time, Holly knew her mum was hiding something. She was sure she was involved in something bigger than it had first appeared. And if her mum was going to hide her head in the sand, it was up to Holly to unearth whatever it was that's happening in her little village. She was quite sure time was running out for Ethan, and perhaps Bette's fate had been somehow linked. Where her appearance all those years ago fitted in, however, needed a little more thought. And she was starting to wonder if she perhaps knew of someone who may have some of the answers.

## CHAPTER 25

# Holly

'GOOD MORNING, SIR.'

'Holly. How pleasant. Are you dropping your brothers off?'

'Yes, sir. They're just gone into class. I wonder if I could have a word.'

The old man nodded. 'Let me just drop this off at the office and I'll be right with you. Shall we walk?'

Holly followed Mr Bartholomew down the wooden floored corridor, and inhaled the familiar beeswax polish smell, unchanged from all those years before. He had been her teacher a few times, in this small village school and Holly had always liked the way he never changed, never raised his voice, was calm and strict and kind all at the same time, and yet commanded such respect from everyone in the school, adults and children alike. Parents and teachers seemed to flock to him and he took everything in his stride, this serious little man who had been there forever. If anyone could help her, he would be the one to do it.

As he handed in the yellow folders over to the receptionist, he spoke quietly and obviously about her, as the girl looked over to her, nodded, and then went back to her desk.

'The staff room is free. Shall we go there?'

'I wondered if we could go down to the garden, sir. I wanted to show you something.'

He nodded, and then motioned to the staffroom door. 'Let's start here, shall we? It's perishing out there today and I have a feeling we may be some time.'

Holly followed him in to oak-panelled room, the upright armchairs faded and probably as old as the old man himself.

'Sit down.'

A shiver ran through Holly as she knew what she had to say wasn't going to be easy. But Mr Bartholomew was such an authority in the village; surely he would know something. Her confidence was deserting her and she wondered if her mum was right, people would think she was deluded, or fantasising, or ill. She pressed her lips tightly together and began.

'Sir, can I ask you something?'

'Anything, Holly. I understand you're having a difficult time at the moment so I'm glad you've come to talk to me. I'll do anything I can to help.'

'You worked with my mum didn't you, years ago?'

The old teacher motioned for Holly to sit down, yet he stayed upright, walking instead to a long sash window, painted shut over the years, its iron frame creamy white.

'That's right, and Ethan's mum – they both trained here, and then your mum continued working here for, a few years, if I remember. She was a breath of fresh air when she joined us. I thought a lot of your mum. She was a very good teacher.'

Holly smiled. Her mum would like that. She had always said teaching was in her blood.

'Do you remember when she found me? Did you know her then?'

'She stopped working around that time, to look after you. She was so thrilled that you had come into her life. She always said you were a blessing. A gift.'

'Was I?'

'Were you what, Holly?'

'Was I a gift? Where was I from? Do you know anything about my mum or the place I came from?'

'You were a gift for your mother. It's a turn of phrase, nothing more.'

'That's what mum says. But don't you think it's strange? That no one ever claimed me? That she'd been so desperate for a child and then, lo and behold, there I was?'

'What are you saying, Holly?'

'I don't know, sir, but you were there then. You were there when Bette disappeared and I appeared. It's just a bit strange, don't you think?'

'I think you are upset about Ethan. I think you are trying to find answers and I know that sometimes when we try to join up the dots, we can create all sorts of reasons for strange coincidences. Leave well alone, Holly. You need to let your mum tell you her truth and trust her. She made sacrifices for you. We all did.' Mr Bartholomew turned back from the window and the morning light silhouetted him creating a glow that shone against the dust motes in the room.

'What do you mean? Sacrifices? What did you do? Do you know where I came from?'

'I think we need to focus our energies on finding Ethan. You wanted to go to the garden, Holly. Shall we?'

'I found Ethan. No one believes me except the librarian up at my school, Miss Sharp. He's trapped by witchcraft or faerie magic— something weird like that. I don't know. But you must know stuff. What's our Healing Garden for if it's not protection of some kind? Please be honest with me, sir.'

'Miss Sharp needs to refrain from filling your head with her fantasies.' He strode over and swept through the door, Holly almost running to keep up with him.

But I wanted to show you something. Can we go down to the garden and the woodland through the gate? Mr Bartholemew?'

He strode on, out of the building, the tails of his tweed jacket flapping after him. Holly scurried after, down the corridors, out on to the playground and down towards the old gardens where he had cultivated the gardens over many years. She could not be sure he had even heard her follow.

'Did you start the gardens?'

The grass squelched, slightly damp from rain the previous night and the early morning dew, but Holly's boots kept her upright and helped her keep up with this sprightly old man who had seemed to cover quite a distance without losing breath.

'In answer to your question, Holly, the gardens were started in response to a request from the parish council many years ago, when I was a young teacher, years before I knew your mother, when the school was run by an old head teacher called Mrs Burrows. A funny little woman–kind yet strict, running her school in the ways head teachers used to run schools, more like a large family home than anything. She was asked to grow a healing garden for the people in the village and our school was the perfect place for such a garden where children could learn about the healing properties of herbs, flowers and grasses, where they may benefit from the protection such a garden could bring.'

'Protection?'

'Many years ago, it was believed that a healing garden had protective powers and of course, children are those we wish to protect the most. It made common sense that the village should set up its healing garden near the school.'

'Protection from who?'

'Can you see these herbs along here? These were planted by your younger brothers, Holly. Just a few weeks ago, and look how they have grown. Your brothers have special gifts too – you must tell them their sage and mugwort are flourishing.' He smiled and walked down to the cartwheel, stuffed with colourful wild flowers and grasses, heathers and herbs. 'You planted some of these as a child. Do you remember?'

'Protection from what, sir? You started to–'

'Holly, the village has always been superstitious. Maybe it's rubbing off on me too. Old magic and folklore, when you live with it all your life, it starts to feel real. But we must keep it back where it belongs, away from our modern world–back in the shadows. Don't bring it into the light, Holly. Too many sacrifices have been made and your mother has warned you too. I need you to listen very carefully.'

'But, sir, you're not making any sense. I'm trying to tell you about Ethan–no one wants to know.'

'It does not have to make sense, Holly. The truth barely ever does.'

Mt Bartholomew walked over to the wall which separated the gardens and the woodland beyond.

'Through there, sir. I wanted to go through there. Do you have the key to the gate?'

He moved towards the gate and rested his head against one of the black wrought iron bars.

'Through there is a place of remembrance. It hasn't been opened for years. The villagers placed flowers on the elm trees year on year at one time. The tradition has died with the last in line of some of the families who lost their young. It was beautiful at one time.'

'Other children died?'

'Over the years, yes. We have the misfortune in this village that from time to time, a child is taken from us. This helps to make some sense of family grief.'

'So this has happened before?'

'Holly. In villages all over the world, children are lost and taken from us every day. We find ways to protect our young yet they still leave us. That is the way of our world I am afraid.'

'But why was Bette taken? Why was Ethan taken? This is different? I'm starting to imagine all sorts of reasons. Please tell me what is happening. What does this have to do with me?'

'Why do you feel you are somehow tied up in all this?'

'The gate. The gate was open yesterday because I came through it. That's what I'm trying to tell you. I was there—and I pushed the gate open. It opened for me and I ran home!'

'Explain yourself, my child.'

'I went to find Ethan at the caves. He was there. He was trapped in the caves so I tried to get help.'

'The police saw nothing, Holly. You were mistaken.'

'No! I went again – he was definitely there. Miss Sharp says it's magic and I know Ethan is in mortal danger. I went to find him, to save him and somehow I ended up in the woods beyond the gate. I had been put there. I know it makes no sense but you must believe me. I – I –' Her mind fogged and her words tangled.

Mr Bartholomew shook his head and walked away. 'Enough, Holly. You are quite grief-stricken. That much is true. The loss of Ethan is almost too much for your poor mind to bear. Once, years ago, we took some flowers to lay there for Bette. Some of the school teachers, we felt it was the only thing we could do. That was the only time the gate has ever been opened.'

'I've been there, sir. I don't know how it happened—'

'No, Holly. You can't get in there. You mustn't. The gate is locked, rust-locked now after all this time and no one has the key.'

Standing there, he seemed to shrink for a moment, his hands clasped tightly in front of him. 'The woodland is said to be cursed. It was a graveyard hundreds of years ago for children who died at the school when it was once a hospital. The trees are elm trees, and they protected the children's spirits, so the story goes.'

Holly nodded. 'Yes! You must believe in this then, to lay flowers when Bette went missing. I'm sure you believe in something other than just this and police and missing children. What is happening here?'

'Go back to school, Holly. You are not to pursue this. Your mum is right. You must let the police look for Ethan and you must be strong. Follow the path your mother has carved for you and do not come back here. You will just cause trouble for yourself and upset for those who love you. Please . . .' He stopped and again shook his head. 'I worry that you will not take heed, Holly. What you think you know and what you really know are worlds apart. Let us protect you. Please. The alternative is too horrible to consider.'

He wasn't making any sense, yet he was starting to sound like her mother. They walked in silence up to school and Holly thanked the old teacher before making her way to school. She was not stupid. She was not to be protected. And while Ethan was still missing, she had to do everything in her power to get him back, if only to bring his body home. And with a stifled sob, she made her way back to school.

## Chapter 26

# Holly

WORD WAS OUT about Ethan. What seemed to be the talk of the day was that Holly had been with the police looking for him and had found his cap down in the caves. As she walked the corridors of school, students she'd never met before wanted to talk to her or at least pat her on the shoulder to say they were either sorry, thinking of her or praying for her, wholly dependent on the groups they belonged to. Of course, the drama crowd were desperate to be part of this, and Holly had become a minor celebrity in their minds overnight.

As she walked with Emma in to the lunch hall, the tables were full of students, refuelling after a busy morning. Their trays betrayed their lack of appetite and held only drinks and suspiciously dry cheese wraps.

'Do come and sit with us, Holly dear, you must be so traumatised after your ordeal.' Clementine was waving them over to the table of beautiful people, all full of their own self-importance and keen to entangle themselves in anything that might boost their popularity.

The girls who flicked their hair and turned up their noses at Holly and Ethan a few weeks before were now keen to pull her in to their inner circle, and Holly was almost embarrassed for them as they tried every which way to have her close. The girls sat down at the end of the table and eyed each other knowingly.

'How are you, Holly?'

'Fine and dandy, Clementine. Fine and dandy.' Holly focused on the dry cheese wrap and noted the grated cheese falling messily onto her plate. She turned her attention to the orange cheese strands and pressed a few at a time on her index finger before eating them slowly and deliberately.

'You can tell us anything, Holly. We're looking out for you now.'

'I don't need looking after, thanks,' she replied with as much courtesy as she could muster. 'I'm just trying to eat my lunch.'

'Did you have to go the police station? I heard that Ethan ran away because his step dad beat him up. A girl at the salon told me and she knows someone who was in his year at school before he got expelled, years ago. Terrible business, that's for sure.'

The girls nodded, their shiny manes barely moving as they urged their friend to go on.

'And - then there's the caves. What was he even doing down there, Holly? Were you with him when he disappeared? We didn't know you were so close.'

They were digging for facts, like little truffle pigs desperate for some titbit to chew over for the next few days until the next drama presented itself.

'Let her eat her lunch ladies,' Emma smiled. 'As kind as you are letting us sit with you, we are just trying to eat our lunch and then we'll go.'

'Of course, of course,' smiled Clementine, yet her smile was one akin to the wolf before it tries to eat Little Red Riding Hood, sat there all sweet and innocent in Grandmother's petticoats and night cap. 'It's just we want you to know we're here for you, Holly dear. You can tell us anything.'

Holly stood up sharply, her seat grating like fingers on a chalkboard. 'Come on Em, we'll just go and sit somewhere else. You really don't need to take me on as your new project.'

Clementine's face fell in mock horror as she looked around her at the group of lip-glossed girls, their hair long and waved, perfect for flicking in bored disdain. 'Well there's no need to be rude, Holly. We only offered you a seat because we care.'

'You only offered us a seat because you are a gang of gossipy girls who think you have the right to anyone's business. Leave me alone and go back to curling your eyelashes or whatever it is you all do to fill the hours between beauty appointments. Unbelievable.'

Holly and Emma moved to the other side of the canteen and sat lightly down next to some students who were busy discussing the latest Dungeons and Dragons move in their card game. Holly smiled.

'Their faces, Holly. You were on form. You do know you won't be getting a sleepover invitation anytime soon?'

'Do you think? I couldn't bear to listen to them a minute longer. Do they really think I'm that stupid not to see through that act? I will never be their flavour of the week or would ever want to be.'

'Good for you, Holly. Now shut up and eat your sandwich.'

The girls laughed and hastily drained their glasses of orange juice before rushing back to class.

CHAPTER 27

# Holly

THEIR DIMINUTIVE TEACHER was on top form again this morning and nodded to the girls as they entered her room. 'Girls, come and sit down and rest your wearies. How are you bearing up, Mistress Holly?'

'I'm okay thanks, Miss,' Holly lied.

'I'm not expecting your homework in today – you can have until the end of the week.'

Holly threw her exercise book lightly on to the top of the growing pile of dog-eared, poster covered books on the teacher's front desk. 'Done, Miss. I was glad of something to do.'

Her teacher pinked slightly adding to the glow of her rouged cheeks and she nodded. 'Take a seat, Holly. Time to see what Lady Macbeth has been up to again.'

Holly was glad to sit back and watch the text come to life as Miss Green wailed at the imagined blood on her hands as a very timid boy called Dominic stood to take the part of the doctor confiding in Macbeth that his new Queen was indeed insane. Dominic's delivery of the lines were comical as he hammed up every line to meet Miss Green's performance, while Teddy Brown, a boy who cringed at the very mention of his name unless to talk about Doctor Who and all things Star Trek, read Macbeth as if he had been turned into one of his revered cyber men. The afternoon passed comfortably by, and Holly was glad of the distraction of her classmates and the untangling of Shakespeare's words and heated debate about their meaning.

It had been a relief not to think about the mess she was in, the danger Ethan was in, and the way all the adults in her life had started talking in riddles. But on her arrival at home that evening, the police car parked outside nearly stopped Holly's heart.

She ran into the house and shouted out to her mum as the door slammed behind her.

'Have they found him? Is he okay?'

At the kitchen table, Ethan's mum, Sally, and her own mum sat together while a police officer across from them scribbled notes frantically in a little note pad evidently too tiny for the job.

'There is some news, Holly, but I'm afraid you need to sit down.'

Holly sank in to the chair closest to her, before her legs gave way.

'They've found him,' she sighed.

'They've found something, Holly', her mum started, 'but I need to go and –' she looked to the police officer for reassurance.

'What have they found?'

'They're not sure,' her mum whispered, looking at the police officer for reassurance. 'Will you be ok here for an hour?'

'Where?' Holly stood up. 'Where is he?'

'Someone has been found in the woods behind your school.' Her mum spoke almost inaudibly and Holly had to strain to hear her. 'Police have widened their search area to include the school grounds and the woods beyond it, Holly. I have to go and identify him.'

Holly turned. 'Why aren't you going, Sally?'

'Sally will go later. I'm going first – it might not be him. Sally's not feeling strong enough.'

Sally sat crumpled in the chair, much smaller that Holly remembered. Holly knew there was nothing she could say and so nodded sadly.

The police officer gestured to Holly's mum and she rose slowly.

Cara sighed and pulled at a stray strand of her hair. 'We'll be back shortly, Holly. Just be careful. Stay here with Sally. That's all I ask.'

Holly made Sally a cup of tea then retreated to her bedroom. It held remnants of Ethan all around the place–a discarded script, crisp packets in the bin, last year's birthday card–which she'd felt kept him close. But she knew. She knew this was not what she had hoped for, but this was what her dreams had foretold. She had known all along that Ethan would not be coming home. Her mum would now need to explain. There was much Holly needed to know.

## CHAPTER 28

# Cara

HIS BODY LAY slumped against the roots of an old yew tree, his arms crossed over his torso, protectively. Dark red clung dry and decorative along one side of his body, in swathes of curved patterns, almost tie-dye in design, yet it was clear to anyone who came close that this had not been a peaceful passing.

Cara's hand rose up to her mouth sharply, stifling a scream as she processed the lifeless body in front of her. 'Oh no,' she whispered, 'Poor Ethan.'

'It's him, then?'

'Yes.'

She stumbled towards him and fell into the wet mossy undergrowth as she stroked his hair out of his eyes in a vain attempt to soothe him.

'You mustn't touch him, Cara. This is a crime scene.'

She shook her head. 'Oh, Ethan, I'm so sorry. Please forgive me.'

'What's that, Madam?'

'There's something I should have done, or not done. A long time ago. I just feel so responsible.' She sobbed as she took in this poor crumpled body, discarded so cruelly, used and thrown out on the scrap heap when he was of no further use.

'You're not making any sense. Do you need to escort me to the station and tell me what you know?'

She laughed inwardly and shook her head. 'No, of course not. Just a mum thing. Ignore me.'

The officer helped her up from the floor. 'The vans are on their way, they need to get on with their jobs. You know how it is. Maybe you could take Holly to the chapel when he's been –' he gestured to the body '– tidied up a bit.'

'It's all such a mess.'

The poor boy's colour was pale, the blood drained from him, his skin a waxy translucent blue. He had obviously been placed there, thrown there, the way his body lay awkwardly on this bed of leaves and mossy undergrowth.

'Well, I've never seen anything like it. The labs will be busy sorting this one out.'

'Can you leave me with him for a moment? I just want to say my goodbyes.'

'We're not allowed to leave the body, but I'll give you a moment. Just don't touch anything, you hear?' The police officer walked away hesitantly, casting a backward glance every few seconds as he went.

With the officer out of view, she put her hand on Ethan's chest and edged up the filthy sweatshirt he had worn that day. That day when he had entered the cave, unaware of how his destiny was already marked out for him, walking straight in to his fate.

The dark red scars were waxy against his pale flesh and marked out the temporary home for another. Something that had lived and since disappeared, leaving Ethan's body an empty shell. Payment for her sacred child. Yet this poor boy, who once had been her daughter's best friend and her best friend's darling son, had died so that some strange being could live and strengthen its kind, to continue the terrible events that she had been tricked into, that she herself had enabled.

'I'm sorry, Ethan,' she whispered. 'If there had been any other way . . .'

She jumped as a nearby rustling startled her from her thoughts. 'I'm finished, Officer,' she started, standing so quickly her head spun as the blood rushed to steady her. 'It's all finished.'

No one was there, just a cold blast around her as she steadied herself against this nearby elm. The rose oil scent was there again and she knew. In that instant she knew Ethan was at peace at last as his sister had come to collect him. But in that moment, she realised that now she would never be at peace again.

## CHAPTER 29

# Holly

THE RAIN HAD beaten on the window glass all night, so heavy was the downpour. Her view from her room, across the rooftops of the terraced housing usually spread away from her in neat lines and repeated angles, yet tonight the colours were wet, bleeding together in the pallet of her window frame, her wet eyes adding to the distortion. The days and nights blurred these days.

She wished she hadn't gone now. She wished she had stayed behind and let her mother bring her the bad news. But already knowing the outcome, it seemed silly to wait around and she had followed them there, waiting in the shadows until the police officer had walked away, leaving her mother fallen down in the muddy leaves next to Ethan, poor dead Ethan, as she cried and pulled at his clothing, sobbing in to her hands as Holly watched, hidden.

But it was as the dark shadow had moved itself across the woodland, as a wisp of grey smoke as it danced from tree to tree, that her mother had jolted upwards to the spirit engulfing her. Holly had almost shouted out in fear yet saw her mother gasp 'Bette!' – a sound which shook the very trees surrounding her and caused the grey smoke to jolt at once away from her mother and towards the body laid out on the woodland floor. As it lay above his body, ebbing towards and away, it again began to form that slight figure of the girl who had once lived and died as her brother had, well before her time, years before. Bette had simply come to collect her brother but had needed to make contact with Holly's mother–to warn her or punish her, Holly was not sure. Then, as Bette's silken silvered frame covered Ethan like a shroud, Holly watched aghast as the two greying figures faded in the twilight. Her mother, too, had watched, her fingers over her open mouth, before walking on towards the officer who had come running, shouting about the lack of evidence: the body, the corpse. Holly watched, hidden, as her mother sobbed, shaking her wild hair, frantically looking around her in a bid to rid her brain of the images playing through her mind and make sense of what she had just witnessed.

Bette. She had been here. Here to collect her brother. Holly's mother knew that and as Holly saw her mother's frantic reaction she wondered if, perhaps, the truth would now reveal itself.

Could her own mother really have known about Bette and Ethan? How had Cara's best friend lost two children during her life while she was able to find and bring up a child as her own? Holly desperately needed to hear some answers. And this time, she needed to hear the truth.

## Chapter 30

# Holly

THE FAMILIAR SMELL of floor polish and Witch Hazel potion, once applied liberally to sting cuts and scratches, followed Holly down the corridor. Standing outside the office door, her stomach clenched nervously. She raised her hand to knock.

There were two voices within–Mr Bartholomew and another, an older female voice–and Holly paused, her clenched hand in mid-air as she listened.

'It is in the past. That is all there is left to say on the matter.'

'The girl is running around getting herself in to all sorts of scrapes. Moon madness has finally claimed her, Henry. I warned you all those years ago.'

'Hysteria is not going to help, Rose. Now calm yourself and head home. I'm not going to ask you to help in the library this afternoon when you're obviously in no fit state.'

'My concern is as it always was. Cara has meddled with things bigger than you or I. There is only so much we can do to protect our children. I fear this is only the beginning.'

'Rose, my dear, you worry so much and that's commendable. Yet we have managed over the years to prevent much trouble and will continue to do so. Poor Ethan was part of the past and now he has gone, we can look forward to a safer future for our children.'

Holly fell forward at the mention of Ethan's name and her fist banged once on the door.

The voices fell silent and a difficult moment or two ticked by.

'Holly!' Mr Bartholomew opened the door and motioned for her to enter. 'How are you, my dear?'

'You must be Cara's daughter.' The other voice had belonged to the old crooked librarian, her face crinkly and pale brown with high pink spots on each cheek, powdered circles placed in perfect symmetry. 'We have met before.'

Holly shifted nervously. 'I came to see you, sir,' she started. 'It's Ethan.'

'We have heard news of his death, Holly. We were so sorry to hear about him.'

'So tragic,' the powdered lady mused, shaking her head. 'Another life taken in the same way. As was foretold.'

'I'm sorry, but I'm unsure what is going on,' Holly frowned.

'Dark forces, Cara,' she whispered, her watery green eyes narrowing. 'We always knew there would be consequences, yet no one dreamed of this.'

'Sir?' Holly moved backwards, as Miss Sharp's crooked frame shuffled closer.

Miss Sharp nodded sadly. 'We've done what we were bid.'

Mr Bartholomew ushered the old lady out of his office. 'Are you sure you are able to work this afternoon, Miss Sharp? Only if you feel up to it. You should really be getting yourself home.'

The old lady shook herself, as if pulling herself out of a trance. 'I'll be absolutely fine, Henry. Do stop fussing.' Miss Sharp nodded to Holly. 'I've been a librarian for so many years, Cara, I'm surprised you don't remember me!'

'This is Cara's daughter, Miss Sharp. This is Holly.'

Miss Sharp rushed forward and took Holly's hand in hers. 'You.'

'Hello, Miss Sharp. We met at my school. You're our librarian.'

'Oh of course. Time ticks by and I forget. Forgive me.'

'I do remember you. I visit the library sometimes. You helped me with some research last week. Do you remember? About changelings and faerie folklore.'

'Oh yes. I'm just a little distracted today. Those little pixies fog my mind sometimes with all their plotting and scheming!'

'Forgive her Holly. She is becoming more and more muddled with each year.'

'You're doing it again, Mr. Bartholemew,' Holly cried. 'Please let me in. Tell me what is happening. I'm so confused!'

Miss Sharp squeezed Holly's forearm gently. 'That is to be expected. All will settle back now, my dear, all will be well. You and little Holly are safe.'

Holly frowned. 'I'm Holly.'

'You and Holly are but one—you will protect her.' Miss Sharp's soft hands gripped Holly's arm tightly.

Holly smiled politely. 'I think you are mixing me up with my mum, Miss Sharp.'

'Of course, of course.' Miss Sharp tapped her nose, conspiratorially and winked. 'Mum's the word.'

'Come on, Miss Sharp, off to your library. There are books to organise!'

The old lady smiled. 'Your troubles are behind you now. Look forward and let the sun warm your face once more.'

Shutting the door, Mr Bartholomew turned back to Holly. 'Miss Sharp is a little eccentric, Holly. She gets very confused these days.'

Holly sat herself down determinedly. 'She seemed to know my mum, sir. She kept calling me Cara.'

'Your mother worked at the school years ago and was close to Miss Sharp when she was our librarian here, Holly.'

Holly's head was spinning. She knew something was not quite right, yet the adults were colluding to keep her out of a situation that obviously involved her. A game of which she didn't know the rules and so kept missing, kept losing. Like an enchanted game of snakes and ladders with snakes that moved squares, catching you when you felt you were safe then sliding down to the very bottom, only to have to start again from the very beginning. She needed to take charge.

Holly crumpled in to the leather high backed chair. 'Who am I, sir?'

'A much loved, a much longed for child, Holly. That is all you need to know.'

'I can't help thinking I'm something to do with Bette and Ethan though. Mum's friend, Sally, lost two children and here I am safe. How can that be fair?'

'Life isn't fair, Holly. Life can be unkind and cruel but it can also be exciting and full of adventure. Try to focus on the life you have and not the lives others have lost. It will drive you to the brink of madness.'

A knock sounded and Mr Bartholomew jumped up. 'Ah, Cara. Come in.'

Cara rushed in. 'Holly, my darling. Are you okay?'

Holly shrugged, her mum's arms loosening and releasing her. 'Not really.'

The two adults exchanged worried glances but Holly had seen it. 'What is going on? You know something about Ethan - my dear friend - who is now dead. Tell me what is happening.'

'They found him, Holly. That's all I know.'

'What did you see, Mum? He had been hurt, hadn't he? When I found him in the caves, when no one seemed to be able to find him, I found him and he was hurt. He had something on him that was hurting him. Did you see it?'

'I don't remember, Holly.' Cara rubbed the skin across her forehead harshly and looked to the head teacher.

'But where did they find him, Mum?' Holly whispered.

'The woods. The woods behind your school,' Mum answered.

Holly jerked suddenly, her nerves on edge and her head spinning. 'Where in the woods?'

'I don't know, Holly. I don't remember.' Cara smiled tightly.

'I followed you there, Mum. You were with Ethan. I saw you. I saw Bette.'

The head teacher shook his head. 'Bette has been gone ten years, Holly. I think you're upset and that's understandable. But now you're hurting your mum too.'

Holly knew that look and narrowed her eyes. 'You know something, Mum. You need to start talking.'

'Bette is gone. Ethan is gone. I feel so sad about it but I can't tell you what you want to hear.'

'Can't? Or won't?'

Mr Bartholomew stood up. 'Take her home, Cara.'

'But, sir—you need to help me get to the bottom of all this.'

'Do not meddle, Holly. You are safe now and your Mum is tired. See that she gets some rest.'

Mother and daughter walked down the corridor. Always so close before, Holly felt distant from her mum, as if brambles had wrapped themselves around her tightly, protectively keeping her safe yet letting no one close.

Cara talked without looking up. 'I went to the woods, Holly, but I didn't see anything unusual. I saw Ethan, poor child, but it was quick and I was led away by the police officer. This is not an adventure story, Holly. Just let the police make a mess of it all again. They don't know what they're doing, quite frankly, and in time, this will pass. We are safe.'

'How can you say that? What if the children are not safe? What if something like this happened to me?'

'You are the safest child in the village, Holly. I made sure of that. Now, I'm tired of all the drama. Poor Ethan is safe now and at rest.'

'Mum, you're lying. I can tell! I was there. I followed you.'

Cara stopped and steadied herself against the corridor wall.

'I saw you with Ethan. Then I saw Bette. You have to tell me what's going on.'

Cara rubbed her forehead wearily. 'I'm going home for a lie down, Holly. I suggest you do too. All this excitement has quite addled your brain. I need you to look to the future and not dwell on the past.'

'But, Mum—'

'Please, Holly. I need this all to stop.'

'What needs to stop? What has this got to do with me?'

Cara closed her eyes and spoke very slowly, the words breathed from her like smoke escaping from a locked door. 'You have been saved, Holly. I made sure of that. There is no more danger. That is all you need to know.'

## CHAPTER 31

# Cara

*S*OFT, DECAYING LEAF *litter carpeted her way. The elm trees robbed her of the bright autumn afternoon and her delicate frame shivered. The shadows moved as she ran swiftly through the trees, time ticking and dusk threatening. Cara had to be home before night fall.*

*As the dense foliage opened out to reveal the clearing, Cara knew she had found the place. The ring of elm trees were stately yet close enough together. The dull, mossy floor, no longer leafy, cushioned her every step. She walked around the circle, the trees watching her every move. At certain trees, almost hidden, lay tiny bouquets of flowers: blue bells, forget-me-nots, lily-of-the-valley, which, on closer inspection, were growing out of the moss in such a way that they looked like some tiny hand had placed them there as if in memory of someone lost or passed on.*

*One tree, its trunk bound with brambles, was starred with tiny white*
*and rosy flowers with a promise of a berry in its centre and at its base lay a*
*mossy boulder, its back to Cara, sleeping.*
  *'Mummy? Mummy?'*
  *The boulder sat up and showed itself. Holly's face turned towards her,*
*mossy and dewy, smiling and sobbing.*
  *'Where is this, Mummy? Where am I?'*

Cara sat up in bed, bolt upright in the darkness. Her dreams were
always the same except that sometimes the face was Ethan, or Bette,
but never Holly. Holly would never be safe until Cara put a stop to this
madness. There, in her nightmares, this image would remain, staining
every sleep with its memory and every following day with its echoes.

Ethan was her undoing. She knew that now. Her promise made
when she so wanted a child had been requested in full. The moon
magic that had given her this beautiful child was now threatening to
destroy the peace of the village, something she had always worked
so hard to protect. When Ethan had been killed, he had been the
start of it all again, Cara could feel it. If she wasn't careful, would she
be asked for more children? And what if she refused? What would
happen to Holly?
  It was time to face Miss Trench and put things right once and
for all.

Cara swallowed hard, a sharp pain rising below her rib cage –
an acid burst of bottled guilt. While Sally's downward spiral wasn't
completely her intention, she knew her actions all those years ago
were somehow linked to Bette's disappearance. And although Cara
had never really been sure what really happened, Miss Trench and
the events surrounding her finding Holly could only mean one
thing. She'd ignored it for so long. She pulled clothes on quickly in
the darkness, yesterday's clothes discarded at the end of her bed,
crumpled and comforting as she wrapped the grey cardigan around
herself. She leaned in to see Holly lay sleeping in her bed, her face
lit gently by the full moon, beautiful yet so vulnerable. Cara hurried
down the stairs, pushed her feet into unlaced boots and slipped out
of the house.

Strange things had occurred around the time she found Holly, things she was never really able to explain, and Cara now knew that her desire for a child all that time ago had triggered a most sinister chain of events.

Cara knew where this woman lived. Yet another secret she had kept. These secrets, her denial to face facts were starting to bubble up to the surface and the truth had to be made clear.

Walking down moonlit hill to the main road, Cara remembered. Running home with Holly wrapped up tightly in swaddling clothes of ivory silk, Cara had known she had been granted her most precious wish yet had never dared to speak of it.

Miss Trench's house stood at the bottom of the hill, just round the corner from where Cara and Holly lived. Her placement had been deliberate, Cara realised. This woman had been on guard the whole of Holly's life, the whole of Bette's and Ethan's lives too. Just waiting. Like a spider in her web.

Cara pushed through the squeaking iron gate and banged on the old wooden door, green flakes of paint crackling under her knuckles.

The old lady opened the door, her eyes bleary, her mouth set. 'You'd better come in.'

Cara saw the woman's eyes flinch and narrow. 'I'll stay here. I need you to tell me about Ethan.'

'Then come in.'

'No. I'll stay here. I really can't leave Holly for long.' Cara took a deep breath. 'I need you to explain.'

'A sad situation. Bette and then Ethan. Two children lost from the same family. A neglectful mother risks so much, Cara.'

'Why do you say that?'

'Her loss you understand. The children are better off dead.'

Cara stopped herself screaming out loud. 'That is a terrible thing to say, Miss Trench.'

The old woman raised her eyebrows. 'How is Sally?'

'As you would expect, Miss Trench. But I need to ask you –'

'Your child, Holly–is she well? She must be becoming a young woman herself now.'

'Yes, she's a blessing.'

'That she is, Cara. And don't you forget that. Maybe you should hurry home to her.'

'Do you have any idea what happened to those children?'

'Cara, stop beating around the bush. If you have something to say, I suggest you spit it out. I do not have the time nor the inclination to drag up the past.'

'You were there at Sally's, when Bette was first born. I remember you. The child cried and you stopped her crying. But she was so quiet afterwards, so different. Then Ethan. You came and then they were different. These children were so full of life and then–'

'Babies change.'

'Then you were at school the day Bette disappeared. You were in charge that day. She was never found, was she? She just disappeared off the face of the earth. And now Ethan - I saw him in the woods and he was mutilated – as if something had been inside him. I'm not sure I should have ever seen him there. There was something about him, like something had been inside him, growing on him. It was revolting and unnatural and I'm unsure what to think. Bette came back for him. Of that I'm sure. And I know that somehow you have been involved all their lives – you've been there over and over, popping up at times when things have happened. It sounds madness, but something strange–supernatural almost–is happening and I know it's all tied up with you.'

Miss Trench dropped her voice to barely a whisper. 'You just need to remember Holly is your reward. We were so pleased when you led us to the children.'

'My reward? What do you mean?'

'Cara. Whatever you think has happened has happened. You don't need me to spell it out to you.'

'I found Holly. I wished for a child, and then I found her. You can't possibly suggest that I am responsible for Ethan and Bette's deaths?'

'No, not at all. You are responsible for their being removed from a neglectful mother. As babies they were chosen. You helped us find them. And for that we will be eternally grateful. Do not underestimate the power you had at that time.'

Cara leaned against the frame of the door.

'But Holly–'

'She is your reward, Cara. Pure and simple. You were blessed with a moonchild for bringing the children to us. Bette gave her to you while Ethan secured her life on earth. You must not worry. The danger has now passed.'

Cara sobbed as the truth washed over her. 'I don't understand.'

'Oh I know you do, Cara. You always knew. We fogged your mind to help you live with this until Holly was safe. She will remain with you now. Your work is done.'

'Holly is safe?'

'The pact was made, the babies were chosen and the children, in time, passed on their strength. Our kind will now grow strong again and your part in this has been played.'

'Your kind? Who are you?'

'The faerie folk will continue to select children, Cara. You have no power over that. This time you just led us to a couple of unfortunates. We always prefer to take the unwanted, the unloved. They are easily forgotten.'

Cara rested her head in her hands and cried. It was all as she had imagined and worse. It was over.

'And Holly?'

Miss Trench smiled. 'Safe. Your moonchild will live out her life in the mortal realm, moon magic in her veins. Should she ever need to, she can call on those powers. I have great hopes for Holly. She is, after all a magic child, a wished for child.'

The price had been so much, but Holly would now be protected. Her fear of losing this precious child could now fade while the pain of others' sacrifice would always remain with her.

Miss Trench stepped inside and began to close the door. 'I suggest you leave. Now. Go home to your daughter and those boys your husband brought with him. Nothing more to be said.'

Cara stumbled a little and steadied herself on the door frame. 'Yes. Of course.'

'Quite the family now, Cara, for someone like you. Be thankful. Every day. This family you have created is protected. Your silence ensures their protection will continue.'

The door shut.

Holly crouched behind the low wall, her arms tightly wound around her knees. The burn in her chest from quieting her breathing had spread to her shoulder blades and she swallowed a cough rising in her throat. Her black boots rubbed her sockless ankle bones, now grazed raw, and her thin pyjamas offered little protection from the cold. She had heard every word. She placed a hand over her mouth and pressed the gasp back inside.

Cara stood alone in the darkness. Grey clouds passed over the moon and she stood looking skywards for a moment. It would be morning soon and she needed to get back home. Home to Holly. Her darling Holly. That was all she could focus on now. Looking back, she saw Miss Trench's hall light switch off. It was over. She slipped out of the gate and walked home, never looking back. The two children had been payment. Pure and simple. Her beautiful Holly was here and they were not. And she would have to be forever grateful.

And as the moon set, the two females walked silently home against the near dawn, one pulling the other by an invisible thread, forever connected by lives created for them, forever linked by the lives they'd unwittingly destroyed.

# Epilogue

*ONCE UPON A winter's night, under a low white moon, a young woman found a tiny baby hidden under frosted foliage. The child was wrapped in nothing more than a sheet of silver muslin and the woman took her in, blessed with this gift after not being able to have a child of her own for so long. The girl had been so tiny, so pale and waif like, so otherworldly that the woman made it her life's work to keep her safe. At all costs.*

Stepping up wet wooden steps, she faltered. The sky was darkening already, casting the crumbling walls in deeper shadows.

Water splashed on to her face and she realised it had been raining. Her wool coat was soaked through and her feet squelched in the mud as she strode up to the castle keep. The walls were taller and better preserved there, and so would shelter her from the onslaught of rain and hail. She pulled up her hood, cocooning herself from the storm and stilled the storm inside her breathing deeply and heavily while her heart tightened with all the bitter feelings she hated. She was turning in to her grandmother she realised, spitefully coveting what others had. 'Stop it, Cara. Pull yourself together!' She shouted in to the rain and turned her face to the wet white stones.

Silver light cast down the grey slime of the old wet rock. It sparkled where the moonlight hit the quartz in the stone and dazzled Cara back in to the moment. How long had she been standing here?

Looking up in to the funnels of raindrops, the moon blurred through her eyelashes and glowed milky and round against the night sky.

'Why can't I have a child? What did I ever do so wrong?' she sobbed, leaning heavily against the rock.

Sometimes, her thoughts would catch her out—so unlike her—lurking deep inside waiting to leap up and out of her at a moment of weakness. She knew she would dote on a child like Bette, she would spend every waking moment worrying, caring, loving, teaching, nurturing—all the things a good mother would do.

Speaking to oneself was a sure sign of madness, Cara was sure. Yet, it felt good shouting into the rain and Cara continued.

'Give me a child, Mr Moon!' she laughed, as wet as could be, her hair, neck and shoulders, thick with water and cold beyond comfort. Her body was shivering, her teeth was chattering, yet she no longer cared. Arms outstretched, the moonlight streaming through this almost horizontal rain now, the wind whistling round the battlements, Cara shouted for one last time. 'Give me my child! You can have anything you like! Just give me a daughter to call my own!'

Sliding down the wall, her boots slipping in the mud, Cara found herself unceremoniously in a heap on the floor, a holly bush preventing a further slide down the hill, wet and muddy as the rain lessened and the wind stilled.

'You're quite mad,' she laughed, 'a single woman up here on her own behaving like some mad old witch!'

The holly bush she had almost tumbled into stood proudly full of red berries and the wind whistled through the prickly green leaves. 'Lead us there.'

'Hello?'

'Lead us there,' the wind whistled again. 'Lead us there and your wish will be granted.'

'Get yourself home, Cara,' she groaned. She did not like the way her mind was racing, knowing full well that Bette was at home now with Sally, neglected and quiet. If only Bette could have been hers, she thought. If only a child could be granted to her, she would agree to anything, such was her desire for her own child.

One day, she would have a child—of that she was sure. The child she often saw in her dreams, her long chestnut hair and those wild green eyes—one way or another. Wishing on a star in the pouring rain was as good a way as any. Star light twinkled through the raindrops catching her lashes, a little brighter for a moment, unless her mind was playing tricks. Warmth spread through her and she fell slowly down to the ground, the dampened grass catching her and holding her there.

A tinkling sound, the laughter of faerie folk, ringing in her ears as she lay there still and soaked through, the star pulsing above her brightly. Time stopped. Just for a moment.

And there she, a baby wrapped in ivory silk as her dreams had foretold. Quiet and gently smiling, she gazed up at Cara, framed by the holly berries, her eyes the colour of the protective leaves.

The seeping cold of the grass made her shudder and she jumped up, her shivering frame painful and wet to the skin. How long she had sat there? Reaching in, she carefully pulled this child towards her, holding her close to her wet body. The child nestled in and slept.

Cara knew then what must pass. And although her heart tightened a little, the moonlight warmed her soul.